W9-BYG-319

Come Juneteenth

Other Novels by Ann Rinaldi

An Unlikely Friendship
A Novel of Mary Todd Lincoln and Elizabeth Keckley

Brooklyn Rose

Or Give Me Death
A Novel of Patrick Henry's Family

The Staircase

The Coffin Quilt
The Feud between the Hatfields and the McCoys

Cast Two Shadows
The American Revolution in the South

An Acquaintance with Darkness

Hang a Thousand Trees with Ribbons
The Story of Phillis Wheatley

Keep Smiling Through

The Secret of Sarah Revere

Finishing Becca
A Story about Peggy Shippen and Benedict Arnold

The Fifth of March
A Story of the Boston Massacre

A Break with Charity
A Story about the Salem Witch Trials

A Ride into Morning
The Story of Tempe Wick

Ann Rinaldi

Come Juneteenth

Harcourt, Inc.
Orlando Austin New York San Diego Toronto London

www.HarcourtBooks.com

Library of Congress Cataloging-in-Publication Data
Rinaldi, Ann.
Come Juneteenth/Ann Rinaldi.
p. cm.
Summary: Fourteen-year-old Luli and her family face tragedy after failing to tell their
slaves that President Lincoln's Emancipation Proclamation made them free.
[1. Family life—Texas—Fiction. 2. Slavery—Texas—Fiction. 3. African Americans—
Fiction. 4. Juneteenth—Fiction. 5. Texas—History—Civil War, 1861–1865—Fiction.
6. Texas—History—1865–1950—Fiction.] I. Title.
PZ7.R459Com 2007
[Fic]—dc22 2006021458
ISBN 978-0-15-205947-7

Text set in Adobe Garamond
Designed by Cathy Riggs

C E G H F D B

Printed in the United States of America

In memory of
Rebecca Leigh Marseglia
May 1, 1988–February 7, 2005

ACKNOWLEDGMENTS

As always, there are no words to express my thanks to the many authors who wrote the factual books on Texas: the lifestyle, the history, and the problems during the American Civil War. Without such research, no writer would be able to even start on such a project as I have undertaken.

I am indebted, also, to my editor, Karen Grove of Harcourt, for her understanding of what I was trying to do, for her input and her patience and her respect for my work. And to my agent, Rosalie Siegel, likewise for her patience and her hand-holding, and sometimes for just listening, which has become, of late, one of the most important chores of literary agents.

Come Juneteenth

PROLOGUE

LAST NIGHT when the fire burned low, when the last of the sweet potatoes under the logs was just a crisp fragrance left of our supper, long after my brother Gabriel had taken his last swig from the flask in his haversack and wiped his mouth with the back of his hand and turned over in his bedroll on the other side of the fire and grunted his good night, last night I lay awake long and unblinking in the spark-filled distance above me. The stars were like pine-knot torches and the moon was brighter than it had a right to be, casting shadows all over the place.

How easy it would be to close my eyes and pretend I was on a hunting trip with Gabriel and Sis Goose, the kind we'd take in the fall after the crops had been brought in and before the first hog killings.

And before the war.

Before we worried about the bluecoats coming. Or how much money Pa was losing not being able to ship all his cotton to England because of the Yankee blockade.

Before we were busy concocting a strange mixture of parched corn, rye, wheat, and okra seed to make our coffee.

Before Gabe went off to guard the northern border and kill Indians.

Before we had to worry about the Confederate states taking a third of Pa's able-bodied negroes to dig fortifications in Galveston. And all I had to worry about then was my next trip with Sis Goose to Aunt Sophie's plantation, which came about either because Aunt Sophie demanded her twice-a-year visits, as Sis Goose's proper owner, or because Sis Goose had committed some serious transgression at home and Mama didn't know what else to do with her.

I was always sent along. Likely because I was part of Sis Goose's mischief and preferred Aunt Sophie's subtle punishments to brother Gabe's out-and-out direct ones.

"Made a mess of things again, hey Luli?" Gabe would say. "Well, now, why don't you come on an' tail after me today and I'll find something for you to do."

"Gabe, I think if I told you . . ."

"Come on now. No time for tellin'." His words were kind, but he would brook no argument. "Lessen you want to go upstairs and see Pa. You want that now?"

Nobody under God's good sun would want that. Pa may be an invalid, but he knows what goes on in every corner of the place. So then I mounted the horse Gabe had waiting for me and rode off around the whole ranch with Gabe to take stock of every broken place in the fences, work until after dusk if need be.

But that time was all finished and done with. And for

me now, too, there was no Sis Goose to snuggle against and giggle with on a trip like this, so that Gabriel scolded.

Sis Goose was gone. Taken from us by the bluecoats. And not by Aunt Sophie as we had always feared would happen. Taken, as sure as an eagle swoops down and takes a rabbit.

Or had she gone of her own free will? If she did, it's my fault. Because of the argument we'd had. I hadn't told Gabe about it. Let him think the Yankees took her. It was easier all around that way.

Someday the truths will come out. Mine and Gabe's and Sis Goose's. We just aren't ready for them yet.

All that matters is that we were here now, under these Texas stars that everybody talks about, to find her. Under these stars that give you no darkness to hide in. And, in the nights that come, or the sun-baked days, we're going to look for her out there somewhere beyond the rim of our firelight. Where, at night, the creatures howl out their apologies for all of us; and in the day, the sun beats down without mercy.

Where the rushes grow on the banks of silver rivers and the blue-eyed grass and wine-cups and star phlox and wild petunias flourish. Where wild boar roam and snakes are in plenitude. And where you don't venture without a rifle and a keen eye for your target.

I had both. Gabe had always insisted upon it. He taught me to shoot at twelve, and I was now as good as both my brothers. It's my vanity, my shot with a gun. I go out into the open and practice for hours sometimes. Lots of times Sis Goose was with me, cheering me on.

She wouldn't touch a gun herself. She is afeared of them.

Out here now, miles from home, you must know what you are shooting at. You must know the difference between outriders and criminals and runaway slaves and Confederate deserters.

Gabe didn't trust me on that. "Wake me before you shoot," he'd said. "There might be others like us out here."

This was my watch, nine until midnight. I had with me the pendant timepiece from Grandmother Heather, Mama's mother, in Virginia. I had often looked at it and wondered if it would keep perfect time out here in this savage land as it had kept the gentle hours in Virginia. It did.

What was it Gabe had said? Others like us? I doubted it. Leastways there was nobody like me, fourteen and equal to the task Gabriel had given me. And him, look at him there, with his faded and worn Confederate uniform the only thing that fits him anymore, its buttons missing, the yellow sash as faded as Confederate paper money, the captain's insignia torn from his shoulders as the bluecoats had demanded. Him, beaten and worn, his wound from a battle with the Kickapoo Indians still hurting him, but no matter. He is ready to cross the Rio Grande, if necessary, to fetch back the girl he loves.

He hasn't seen her since he came home from the war.

She was already gone by then. Does he know she is carrying his child?

There is the question that looms over us like the wingspread of a swallow-tailed hawk. I haven't told him. I promised Sis Goose I wouldn't.

We don't speak of her anyway. He speaks about Kickapoo Indians a lot, especially one woman whom he'd unintentionally wounded when she was pregnant. After, her name had been changed to "One Arm Sleeps" and everyone helped her. He spoke about her in bits and pieces. It happened while he was stationed at Fort Belknap on the Brazos River, where his job was to keep Indians from attacking frontier settlers.

He'd changed with the war. Something had gone out of him and something new had taken over. Some sense of loss, of guilt.

Does he blame himself for not telling Sis Goose she was free these last two years? What kind of man doesn't tell his woman a thing like that?

What would they say to each other when, and if, they meet again? That the choice to tell her she was free was not his to make? If he let that cat out of the bag half of Texas would be in an uproar, expecting a slave uprising. It was that simple.

Of course I couldn't blame his long silences all on the slavery thing. He had killed Indians. Mothers and children. I suppose that is enough to put any man of conscience and honor to shame.

I had never been afraid of him. And I cannot say that about my brother Granville, who never let little things like conscience or honor get in the way.

After all, it was Granville who discovered a way to ship cotton out when nobody else could. He'd arranged things in the small quiet village near the mouth of the Rio Grande on the Mexican side, so cotton could be shipped to England. They say that at any given time seventy ships stacked with bales of cotton could be lying at anchor in the harbor off Bagdad, Mexico. And he'd run the Yankee blockade, too, bringing items we needed home to us.

Nobody in the family questioned Granville's doings. "It takes men like Granville to build empires," Pa had said.

So yes, I was a little bit afraid of Granville and what he'd become. He didn't care. He wanted it that way.

Now, thanks to the war, I was a little bit afraid of Gabe, too. We both knew, of course, that that little bit was too much. But neither of us knew how to fix it.

And so we just let it lie there between us while we attended to other things.

I PUT MORE wood on the fire and gave in to remembering Sis Goose as she was on one of our visits to Aunt Sophie. We'd gone because Aunt Sophie demanded of Mama two weeks a year that Sis Goose visit. When we got there we found out that Lexxy, who served at table, was down with the bilious fever. Right off, Aunt Sophie told Sis Goose,

"Go on, get changed, you must wait on the table tonight. You might as well learn. It could serve you well someday."

The worst part was that she made Sis Goose wear her hair under a turban. She had Suzie in the kitchen do her up. And so there went the long, flowing hair, hidden from sight. And there was the rough, dun-colored dress covered with the whitest of aprons.

Thank heavens there were only three of us—Aunt Sophie, myself, and Uncle Garland—at the table. I did not want to remain. I wanted to be excused, but Aunt Sophie said no. And the next thing I knew, in came Sis Goose with the platter of meat held in her slender hands. And there were tears in her eyes, but she performed her tasks as directed by Aunt Sophie.

"Don't let Aunt Sophie bully her" were Gabe's last words to me before we left. And I promised I wouldn't. For I must mention here that by this time I knew about their secret liaisons, knew how he was smitten with Sis Goose.

And here I was, sitting at table, scared as a kitchen mouse. The food tasted like sawdust in my mouth. I do not know how I got through supper.

Later, in the room we shared, I found Sis Goose crying. "Why does she treat me like a slave?" she asked me.

"It's her way. It's Aunt Sophie. It's why Mama wouldn't let her have you."

"Do you know what she meant by it being good for me to learn to serve at table?"

"No," I'd answered.

"She meant if she died, she has it in her will that someone else should inherit me, and they might treat me as a slave. And if I couldn't do household things, they'd make me work in the fields. That's what she meant!"

She started to cry. I held her. Where was Gabe in all of this? When I saw her with him, though they tried to keep their feelings a secret, I felt like I was a witness at God's creation, they went so well together.

She was "high yellow" in color, or "bright." She was near as white as I.

God's experiment. God's mistake.

"She has papers saying I'm a slave," she said of Aunt Sophie.

"If she does," I said lamely, "I've never seen them."

"I won't stay here," she said, wiping tears from her chiseled face. "I won't be treated as a slave. I'll die first."

"We won't ever let you," I said, taking her hands in my own. They were ice cold, yet her face looked feverish.

She looked at me. "When that negro man came into the barn at home, he said all negroes were free. If what he says is true, I need to know."

That again. The man in the barn. I was warned by both of my brothers to put the incident out of my mind. It had never happened. And if I said it did, one or both of them would convince Pa that I would be ten times better off at Miss Vincent's Academy for Young Ladies, an elite boarding school back in Virginia.

And Pa would be convinced. He always listened to my brothers.

So I never mentioned the man in the barn again. And so I had to face Sis Goose when she mentioned it and tell her that what the man had said was not true.

I had to lie to her, my sister, my friend who'd always been there for me as I was growing up. Who'd taught me to walk and say words. Who'd played at dolls with me and was never jealous of the attention given to me by my brothers.

I lied straight to her face. Right into her liquid brown eyes.

"What the man in the barn said is not true. The slaves are not free. But not to worry. You're not a slave, anyway. And who pays attention to a little old piece of paper that might say so?"

WHEN GABRIEL found out how Aunt Sophie had treated Sis Goose, he was fit to be hog-tied. Gabriel isn't given to anger quickly. Instead he does a slow burn, like a sweet potato in the fire, becoming more ready to explode with each minute.

He was just about to leave for the end of his furlough when he found out. And on the way back to Fort Belknap, he stopped at Aunt Sophie's place to register his complaint.

"You have taken away from her what it took Ma years to build," he told Aunt Sophie.

"Don't you come tramping into my home and telling me what to do, young man," she said. And she gave him what for, as if he were a little boy and not standing in front of her in the uniform of a captain in the Confederacy. "Mind your own business, or I'll be forced into taking her back. Did it ever occur to you that if tragedy struck and we had to sell her, she has no training in household duties at all? And could be put in the fields?"

"She is my business," Gabe told her. But no, it hadn't occurred to him. Or to any of us.

"Just how does she get to be your business?" Aunt Sophie asked. "I hope you're not talking about what I think you're talking about."

Gabe turned on his heel and left for Fort Belknap. The Kickapoo Indians he was up against back there were easier to deal with. Even a fox knows when it is outwitted and will creep back into its lair and lick its wounds and plan for next time.

CHAPTER ONE

I WAS IN the pumpkin patch, counting the ones that were good enough for Old Pepper Apron, our cook, to make into bread. I recollect that Pa was happy that he'd gotten one or two cents more on the pound from the cotton Granville had shipped out of Bagdad. And that the fields were being sown with winter oats and rye.

I looked up and saw Sis Goose standing by the gate, a frown on her lovely face. It was all like some Dutch still life I was learning about from my tutor. Sis twisted her apron in her hands. She always wore a snow-white apron, like I did, even though we had no real household chores.

"Luli, there's an old negro man in our barn," she said.

For a moment I did not understand. The place was full of negro men: field hands, household help. But the look on her face told me something was amiss.

"Who is he?"

"Says he comes from Virginny. Says . . ." and her voice broke.

"Says what?"

"Says the negroes are free. That Abraham Lincoln freed them in January of '63."

That rumor again. But with the war there was a different rumor every week. I swallowed. Something on Sis Goose's face bespoke her distress.

"Go and get Gabe," I told her. "He'll know what to do."

Gabe was in the house, helping Mama decide whether the one hundred bushels of corn she wanted to trade for three pounds of sugar was worth it.

I went to the horse barn, but I didn't go in until Gabe and Sis Goose came back.

"Where'd you come from, Uncle?" Gabe asked the man, who looked old enough to be somebody's grandfather.

"Virginny. I comes from Virginny," came the answer. "From Applegate I come. On the advice of Miz Heather."

Applegate was my Virginia grandmother's plantation.

Gabe scowled and ran his hands over the back of the man's mule. It had USA branded on its back. "This is a fine-looking animal. Where'd you get it?"

"Miz Heather give it to me. And say to come here. She give me a message for y'all."

"What message?" from Gabe.

"She say that no matter what, I shud tell y'all that Mister Linkum done freed the slaves nigh over a year ago now."

"Did she now?" Gabe's voice was tight, forced in its casualness. "Well, to my knowledge my grandmother never had a mule with USA branded on its back. This mule is government property," Gabe told him.

"I came from Virginny," the old man insisted. "Miz Heather, she tell me . . ."

"Yes, yes, I know, that Mr. Lincoln freed the slaves. I'll tell you what, Uncle—" Then Gabe stopped and looked at us. "Go on into the house," he directed us. "Tell no one about this. I'll handle it."

We obeyed. I said nothing to Sis Goose about it. But she did to me. "Do you think he's right?" she asked.

"I don't know. I mean, we would have heard. If not us, then Gabe or Granville. I'm sure we would have heard."

And so I lied to my best friend, my sister, who trusted me. Because I *had* heard of this before. But both Gabe and Granville had ordered me not to speak of it.

The slaves free! I could not think on it all at once. It assaulted my spirit. It gave lie to everything I knew in my life.

All Pa's people in the fields could put down their hoes and walk off if they wanted to. We'd never have another corn or cotton crop. The sweet potatoes and white potatoes and vegetables needing dirt banks to keep them safe from the winter would all be ruined. No more corn shuckings with banjo playing and cider. No one to repair the fences, see to the livestock. In the house, no one to keep Mama's Chippendale furniture free of dust or polish the silver or make the beds. Who would do the laundry?

My mind gave way to hopelessness. And then I remembered what Granville had said the last time a man came to the barn like this. In June of '63, it had been, right before Gettysburg.

"You breathe a word of this and you'll start bloodshed in Texas," he warned me.

Granville liked to make dramatic statements like that.

"I could be free." Sis Goose stopped walking and looked at me. The news had come over her the same way.

"And what would you do?" I asked casually.

She lowered her eyes. Then looked at me almost flirtatiously. "I'd marry Gabe."

No, I couldn't take this, too. I drew in my breath. I'd noticed of late the way he served her at the table before he served himself. How he gave her the best cuts of meat. How he held out her chair. Was he just being a Southern gentleman?

He didn't do all that for me. With me he was brusque, moody. Gentle but sealed off. *Fool,* I told myself. *You should have seen it.*

"Has he asked you?" I pushed.

"Yes. But I can't, unless I'm free. I told him yes, at the end of the war. He wants to marry now. Because he says then Aunt Sophie can't sell me. I'd be his wife. But I don't want to be like my mama, the colored wench of a white man."

She spoke fast. And I thought fast. I entered into a covenant with myself then, a promise to lie, even if it killed me. "Well, it's just a rumor. I'm sorry, Sis Goose. My brothers and my pa would know if it were true."

She accepted that. "You'd never lie to me," she said. "Remember, we're sisters."

CHAPTER TWO

THERE ARE, as far as I can see, two kinds of lies in this world. There's the kind I tell Mama when she asks if I've been to see the hoodoo woman who lives on our plantation. And I say no. Though I have been. And now, like Sis Goose, I have a red flannel bag of my own that holds small animal bones, powdered snakeskin, horsehair, ashes, dried blood, and dirt from the graveyard. All to protect me from any evil I can imagine. And some that I can't.

Then there's the kind of lie you live when you enter into a devil's agreement with yourself never to disclose a certain fact for fear of the results if you do.

There are planters in our neck of the woods who believe so much in the lie that the slaves are not free that they will shoot or hang anybody who says otherwise. And that's what Gabriel knew would happen to Uncle Charley, the negro in the barn, if he were allowed to roam free telling his story. He'd be hanged or shot on the spot.

So Gabriel supplied him with food and money and clothing and sent him on his way, warning him to get out of Texas.

Some planters, like Isaac Coleman, across the valley, and Uncle Garland, husband to Aunt Sophie, would have called a meeting of all his slaves if someone like Uncle Charley showed up at their plantations. And told them it was an outrageous lie. The slaves were not free.

What did slaves on our plantation and other farms think of it all?

Oh, they knew about the war, all right. They called it "the freedom war." And they talked about it amongst themselves. What they would do if push came to shove and they really were free, nobody knew. Likely nothing. They didn't have the means to do anything. It was just easier to pick up the hoe in the morning and go into the fields. To have Massa dole out the weekly supply of cornmeal and sorghum. To be given your winter clothing and see to it that your cabin was chinked up for the cold weather and settle down to enjoy a supper of possum, cooked just the way you liked it.

True, here and there a slave couldn't wait for this freedom anymore. And it wasn't something they heard about from anybody. It was something that grew inside them, all the while they were hoeing or eating that possum. And they would run off, into the river bottoms or the canebrake or the woods, and somehow make their way across the Rio Grande into Mexico, where they would be free.

So far, none of our people have done that. Maybe because Pa treats them good. Maybe because where we are, just east of Austin, Texas, it's many days' journey to the Rio Grande.

And not many strangers who could bring the news come here. Our plantation, called Dunwishin', provides us with everything we need, except what we used to import from England, of course. And all that has stopped with the Yankee blockade. Except for certain goods that Granville can smuggle through to us.

As of now, Mama and I and even my hoity-toity sister, Amelia, are back to wearing homespun for our daily tasks, like my grandmother, Pa's mother, wore when she came here. But thanks to Granville, Amelia's wedding dress was going to be silk. What deals he had to make to get that silk nobody has asked him.

So, even though we've been deprived of things like imported fabrics, leather goods for shoes, and coffee, we get along just fine, thank you. Without the outside world coming to our door and telling us that our negroes should be free.

All this in my favor, it still doesn't forgive the lie I had to tell Sis Goose. Because even though my mama still has papers saying Sis Goose is a slave owned by Aunt Sophie, even though her father was white riverboat captain Ashbel Smith and her mother was a black slave, she was raised free. Simply because Pa wanted it that way. And so she could be a sister to me.

The lie I had to tell her haunts me every day. And when she finds out, I don't know what mayhem it will bring. Maybe she'll never speak to me again. Oh, I'll deserve her wrath, and when it comes I'm half ready for it.

What I find surprising, though, is that, being raised as free, it would bother her so much that the authorities still consider her a slave. I know that in the outside world she could be sold on the block. But this isn't the outside world. This is our home.

Here we can tell as many lies to each other as we need to and still be all right. The thing I don't understand about freedom is . . . can they really take it away from you? And if, inside you, where it matters, you think you are free, doesn't that count for something? Does it have to be legislated to be real?

And then there is another question. How does my brother Gabe fit into this problem with Sis Goose? If he loves her, isn't his lie greater than mine?

I don't dare think of these things. They don't add up. I'd rather go into the pumpkin patch and count the pumpkins to be made into bread. They do add up, and you can't dispute the numbers.

CHAPTER THREE

MAYBE IT'S time now to tell how Sis Goose came to live with us. Maybe that will explain things better than anything.

The year was 1848, and Mama and Pa were living here at Dunwishin' with three children: Granville, who was eleven; Gabriel, ten; and Amelia, just nine. The plantation was thriving. Pa raised a goodly amount of sugarcane back then, but in April a killing frost finished off most of his corn crop. Still, he'd been selling cotton to England steadily, so by the time the war broke out he had two hundred and fifty thousand dollars waiting for him in English banks. Money he couldn't reach during the war. But he still had it.

That year of 1848, Sis Goose was born. But not to Mama.

That was the year Mama's younger sister, Sophie, came to Texas, to the Gulf of Mexico on a steamboat. She was to be married to a wealthy and important man who was the United States minister to England and France. Garland Prescott owned four plantations and four hundred slaves. Mama traveled with her personal girl, Melindy, south to meet Aunt Sophie, who was to stay at our place for two months until the circuit preacher came around to wed them.

Mama, with Melindy, was invited aboard the steamboat *Yellow Stone* for some festivities. On board was a negro woman named Molly, who'd just given birth to a little girl. Aunt Sophie had taken charge of the birth, as she was wont to do. But Molly was dying, and because Aunt Sophie was the only one on board who was really kind to Molly, that negro woman gave the baby to Aunt Sophie before she died.

Molly named her Rose. Her daddy, the captain, was Ashbel Smith, and he promptly signed the baby over to Aunt Sophie.

Her daddy called her Sis Goose.

He knew that by law the baby took her mother's condition of slavery. He knew the oral traditions of the South, too, his mammy having raised him on Brer Rabbit stories.

"As they say in the stories, in the Brer Rabbit tradition," he told Aunt Sophie, "she'll be jus' 'er common goose in de cotehouse when all de rest of de folks is foxes."

So she was called Sis Goose by everyone. And though we weren't all foxes in the courthouse, she was always regarded as a common goose by society.

She was a slave.

Aunt Sophie came to Dunwishin' with her, and Mama took over when Sis Goose cried in the middle of the night, when she wailed out her miseries and her hunger. Mama appointed her a wet nurse from the quarters, and before long she fit into the scheme of things like a bale of cotton packed for market.

Meanwhile, Aunt Sophie was having dressmakers sew her silk and tulle gowns for when she had an audience with Queen Victoria on her wedding trip. By the time she and Uncle Garland were wed, that baby was Mama's. Sis Goose had eyes for no one else but Mama. She smiled only at Mama. She stopped crying only when Mama held her.

"You keep her, Luanne," Aunt Sophie told her. "When I'm settled, I'll come and fetch her home."

But Aunt Sophie never did settle down. If it wasn't a trip to England, it was a trip to Russia where she met the czar and czarina. Or the south of France in the middle of the winter. Or she was entertaining lavishly at their main plantation, Glen Eden. And her stuffed shirt of a husband didn't want Sis Goose. Or if he did, it would be only to have her raised as a household servant.

Mama said she'd run back to Virginia with Sis Goose first. The baby was that adorable with her beautiful smile that made her eyes light up, her pert nose, and golden skin. Everyone knew back then that she was going to be a beauty.

Three years after Sis Goose was born Mama had me. Aunt Sophie and Uncle Garland never did have children. But the year I was born, Pa came down with cholera, and has been in a weakened state since. Mama had to take over running the place with the help of Sam, the negro foreman. The years went on, Granville and Gabe went east to the states, as we call them, to college, and soon enough came the war.

All Aunt Sophie ever demanded was that Sis Goose and I spend two weeks a year at her place. And always there was the implication that she might claim her. Take her away from us. We lived with that fear, especially Mama.

I thought it cruel of Aunt Sophie to do so. And I know by now that if she ever exercised her legal rights and took her, Sis Goose would run away.

"And then what?" I asked Gabriel one day.

"Be caught and sold as a slave by some conniving, stealing man," he said.

Oh, my head spins, thinking on it. And I prefer, on most days, not to think of it at all.

CHAPTER FOUR

I SHOULD TELL some good things before I go on. I mean about our family and how we came to live here. And how my grandfather had to shriek and throw things in the air and yell out to the world that this land was his in order to claim it.

We're not yeomen farmers, with fewer than ten slaves. Neither are we small planters with ten to fifty slaves. Before the Yankees came, Pa had over seventy negroes working the fields and the gardens and tending the sheep, the horses, the cows, and the house. Pa was someone to be reckoned with, not just an ailing old man.

He was already in college in the states when his father, Grandpa Holcomb, came from Virginia as part of that group of Stephen Austin's original "old three hundred" families in that first community of settlers that came to East Texas in 1821.

Edom told me and Sis Goose all this. Edom is close to ninety by now and lives in the log house that is the first one Grandpa built before he built the big one. The same log house all of us live in now that the Yankees came this past June of '65 and put us out of the plantation house.

Edom was in his early forties then, and was Grandpa's body servant. He told us how Grandpa claimed his land. To me, it's so romantic that I never tire hearing tell of it.

In order to take possession of the land, Edom says, Grandpa had to have three witnesses and a surveyor. Stephen Austin was there, too.

The surveyor walked the landmarks with Grandpa, from a red oak tree two feet in diameter, to a pecan tree, to an ash tree, and finally an orange tree. The surveyor dutifully marked it all down.

Then, in order to take possession, Grandpa had to cry out, pull up weeds, throw stones, drive in stakes, and perform other necessary solemn acts to show the land was his.

Exactly the kind of thing I want to do when I'm out riding and I see the endless land and sky. I feel like crying out and pulling up weeds and throwing stones, too. My spirit quickens and I know how Grandpa felt.

Grandmother was with Grandpa when all this happened, of course, on her tall gray horse, Smokey. She'd ridden that horse clear across the country, using a sidesaddle Grandpa had given her. She wasn't afraid of anything. Not Indians or wolves or outriders. And she could shoot a coin off the top of an apple without disturbing its skin. Gabe says I take after her with my shooting and my spirit.

Pa was there, too, when Grandpa claimed the land. It was just before they sent him back to college in Virginia. Grandpa chose a high bluff to build the plantation house on, but first he had to build the log cabin. He built it with logs right off the property. There is a huge fireplace inside. The door shutter is made out of thick slabs split right off the thick pieces of lumber. And the door was locked at night with a large peg that could not be broken through. This was in case of a raid by Indians.

The Indians did come, of course. After all, this was their land. Kickapoos, like the ones who plague our frontier, the ones who wounded Gabriel, would come and walk around the log cabin at night, hoping to scare the wits out of Grandmother. But all she did in reply was take out her spinning wheel and keep it whistling all night so they would be sure to hear it.

Edom told us that before their final leave-taking, they built a fire on the lawn, right where Ma's orchard is now, and danced around it in honor of Grandmother and her courage.

That sure made me proud. And whenever Gabe scolded me, he always put in how nobody would ever build a fire for me in honor of my courage, just to make me feel bad.

Anyway, after the Indians left Grandmother and Grandpa, the buffalo came. A whole drove of them passing through the river about a mile above our house. Grandmother figured there must have been close to a hundred of them, and they never stopped. They went over the land like a flood, and they went southward, Grandmother said.

Those first years were a trial for Grandmother and Grandpa. They had about eighteen head of cattle, a small herd. They'd started out with more, but on the trip west the cattle got sick and some died. They had only six horses left. And they set about the task of surviving.

When the buffalo and Indians weren't plaguing them, the flies and mosquitoes were. Then one year Grandpa's corn crop failed. The next year there was a drought. The year the corn crop failed they had no bread, not until Grandpa raised a good corn crop.

They had no salt at all. But the cotton crop gave a good yield. The only problem was getting it to its destination.

The first few years, before he built his own landing on the river, Grandpa took the cotton to Mexico on pack mules.

Edom told us of this, too: "One slave could manage ten or twelve pack mules. The cotton bales weighed seventy-five or eighty pounds each. The only roads were Indian trails. But we managed eighteen or twenty miles a day."

He told us how the men were heavily armed. And how they hoped the Indians were too afraid of the colored slaves to attack. How, in Mexico, Grandpa exchanged his cotton for coffee, tea, clothing, and Mexican silver dollars.

Pa still has a cache of those silver dollars. I have three. I know my brothers and Amelia have their share, too.

I think about all this because I know how difficult it was for Grandpa and Grandmother to build up this plantation. And because now the Yankees have it. They just took it. And I dream of the day we can get it all back.

"What will it take?" I've asked Gabe.

"Words," he'd said. "Isn't that what it always takes?" And somehow I felt he wasn't just talking about the plantation, and I was treading on dangerous ground, so I shut my mouth right up.

CHAPTER FIVE

THERE ARE more good things I should tell, and I keep them packed away in my memory in a box with a big red bow on top.

I suppose, over the years, I have always been considered as "belonging" to Gabe by the family. And this was long before Pa got so sick he took to his bed and Ma took over the running of the ranch.

You would think the responsibility would fall to Amelia, but she took no interest in me other than to scold. Oh, she oversaw my piano lessons. With a ruler. She smacked my hands with it when I hit the wrong note. I recollect Gabe coming by one time and taking the ruler out of her hands and saying that Chopin didn't learn that way.

Even back then he was protecting me.

I think I was five and he was eighteen and just finishing up college back east. Granville was finished already. Gabe traveled home from the states, part of the way by the rails. Granville was nineteen. Amelia was a little bit jealous of them both, just because they were boys.

When I think about it now, it all falls into place and makes sense. Gabe was the only one who could get me to take medicines when no one, not even Mama, could. He'd fish a candy out of a carefully folded napkin in his shirt pocket and lay it down on the table between us and say it was mine if I would first take the foul-tasting stuff.

He was the one who put me on a horse and taught me to ride, under instructions from Pa, who said it was time. Sis Goose already knew how to ride. Granville had taught her. But she wasn't especially fond of it. And now she was jealous because Gabe was to teach me.

He did such a good job that Pa more or less turned me over to him and made him accountable for me. And when I did something wrong, like leave my horse's tack out in the rain, he, not I, got called on the carpet for it.

He taught me how to shoot, of course, how to clean a gun, how to prepare a wild turkey for cooking, things that Amelia had kittens over.

Things Sis Goose wanted nothing to do with.

I did get him in trouble once, too. When I was about six, Granville told me a story about lions and I was terrorized. I started seeing lions under my bed at night and so did the natural thing.

I got up and went down the hall to Gabe's room, with my favorite blanket, and got into bed with him.

Well, you would think I was the devil himself, tucking his green tail under the covers. Gabe woke in a start and said, "What in the hell are you doing here?"

I told him there was a lion under my bed. And he quickly got up, put on his slippers, and carried me back to my room, where he lighted a lamp and showed me there were no lions under my bed and, satisfied, I went back to bed and to sleep.

The next night my lion returned. And so did I, to Gabe's bed with my blanket.

The same routine. Only the next morning he took me by the hand and found Ma straightening her linen closet.

"Ma, I have a problem," he said. And he told her what it was.

She wasn't alarmed. She simply said she would think about it. Which meant she would bring the matter to Pa. And before you knew it, Gabe's worst nightmare came true. He was called into Pa's study and the door was closed.

I waited outside, with my blanket, and listened.

"Young man," Pa said sternly. "What's this I hear about Luli in your bed?"

"Gawd, Pa, it isn't like that." Gabe sounded miserable. "She sees lions under hers and is frightened out of her wits and comes to mine. I put her back, right off."

"Hmmph," Pa said. "You never think of locking your door?"

"Pa, I couldn't do that to her."

"Well, you *are* going to do it. Tonight. Hear me?"

"Yes, sir." Now he was more than miserable. And I got up and left. With my blanket.

Gabe did not dare disobey Pa. So he did lock his door. And the next morning they found me with my blanket, asleep in the hall on the floor outside Gabe's bedroom.

Gabe couldn't abide that. So he took his pillow and blanket and went out to the bunkhouse where the nigra ranch hands slept and found a bunk and bedded down there. He left the door of his bedroom open.

I slept in his bed. Nobody found out where he was sleeping until days later. When he came into the house, just to eat or change or wash, he wouldn't say a word to anybody. Pa told me to leave him be. So I did.

He wasn't shaving because he was so unhappy, I suppose, and he had at least four days' growth on his face. And it was the first time Pa allowed him at the table in his work clothes. Ma said if he didn't shave soon she wasn't going to allow him at her table anymore. "Yes, ma'am," he said. Poor Gabe.

"Look what you did to him," Sis Goose hissed when we were alone. "It's your fault. All yours."

"See what you did to your brother?" Pa asked. "And he's so good to you."

"I want him back in the house," I sobbed.

"You going to stay out of his bed? You going to get rid of those lions of yours?"

"Yes, sir."

"Well, we'll see. Tonight."

As it turned out, Granville helped me get rid of the lions. After all, this was his fault, he admitted, and it was a family crisis, and when it got right down to it, everybody in my family loved crises. But first Granville sat me down and told me that the only people who slept together in a bed were married, like Ma and Pa.

"Why?" I asked.

He squirmed a bit. "Because that's how it is. Those are the rules. Now look, my story was made up and there are no lions in Texas. They're in Africa. Far away."

But just to make sure, he came to my room and "exorcised" my lions. He did some of what Grandpa did when he claimed his land. He stamped his feet. He ripped up paper; he cried out; he rolled my marbles; and he performed other necessary acts, such as getting down on his knees and chanting to the lions that they had better leave or terrible things would happen to them.

I must say he was good at it.

And that night Gabe came back. He was cleaned up. Whitest of shirts, suspenders, cravat, clean-shaven face, all of it. He didn't say anything to me about the whole affair. That night at the supper table he just acted as if nothing ever happened, and when bedtime came I kissed him good night as if nothing had happened. But I lay awake in my room until I heard my elders coming to bed, until I heard the boys' boots on the stairs, and heard Gabe go to his room and not lock the door.

No lions came that night. And if they had, I would have suffered their growls, their bared teeth, their bites, and my own dripping blood, rather than go to Gabe's room. Because, of all people, Granville had somehow instilled forever in me the rules about people sleeping together, though I knew no more than before. Just the look on his face told me all I needed to know. And the next morning at breakfast Gabe winked at me. To think he'd gone to the bunkhouse to sleep, rather than lock his door against me and leave me sleeping on the floor. Or give the affection we had for each other a bad name. I don't think I ever adored him so much.

To think that Granville had come to my aid, Granville who, at twenty, was already above it all and distant and just a little bit jealous of what I had with Gabe . . . I don't think I ever loved him so much, either.

THERE WERE times, too, when Gabe and I got into mischief together. I particularly recollect the incident of the onions in the stew.

No, Gabe would never outright disobey Pa, and he always reverenced him, but there were times when he teetered on the edge and gave in to boyish impulses, and this time he took me with him.

It was simple. Pa hated onions. Now this may be unseemly for a Texan because most Texans like spicy food, but Pa always hated onions in his food. Ma had to be careful how she cooked, when she did cook, and had Old Pepper Apron trained not to put onions in the stew or the sauces or the salads. Pa's "system," she said, couldn't take them.

The boys missed the onions. They had always had them "back in the states" at school. Oh, Old Pepper Apron made them special salads, but still, a pot of stew bubbling over the hearth on a cold day tasted just as good with or without onions.

Gabe had an ongoing argument with Ma that if she chopped the onions real tiny, Pa and his "system" wouldn't know the difference. Ma held that they would.

This was the spring Fort Sumter was fired upon. I was ten. Sis Goose was thirteen. The war hadn't yet officially started, and Pa and the boys could still disagree over something like onions and consider it worthwhile. This was back before Gabe was killing Indians and Granville was shooting Yankees.

It was a chilly day and Old Pepper Apron was down with some malady. Ma was cooking a stew and it was just starting to bubble on the hearth. She had left me in the kitchen to stir it every so often while she and Sis Goose took some chicken broth to Old Pepper Apron in the quarters.

Gabe appeared in the kitchen doorway.

"This is too good to be true," he said.

"What?"

"I can prove my point today. I can chop up an onion, real small, and put it in the stew, and Pa will never know. What do you say? Are you with me? If we get caught, I'll take all the blame."

"Where will you get the onion?"

"From the root cellar. Others eat around here. The servants use onions. You just keep sitting there and I'll be back in a minute."

And he disappeared. True to his word he was back with one onion, which he commenced to chop up in the most tiny pieces while he told me to keep an eye out for Ma. I did.

I never saw such tiny onion pieces. Where did he learn how? "Sometimes," he said, "when I'm out on the prairie, searching for runaway cows for Pa, and I camp out overnight, I shoot a wild turkey and roast it. I fry up a potato I bring along with a wild onion. Lord, it's good. Even the dog I bring along with me loves it. Now there." And he scooped all the onion off the wooden table and dropped it into the beef stew.

"Stir it," he ordered me. "Do your part."

I giggled and did so.

"Now remember. Don't say a word to anyone. Especially Sis Goose. Don't act strange or laugh or anything. Don't stare at Pa or he'll know something's going on. Hear me?"

"Yes." I said. And I could scarce wait for supper.

AMELIA WAS the first to remark on how good the stew was. "Ma, you're going to have to teach me how to make a stew like this before I get married," she said.

"You getting married?" asked Granville. "When? Can I have your room for an office?"

Those two were at it constantly. For some reason, Amelia did not get on with her brothers.

"Leave your sister alone," from Pa.

He was enjoying his stew. He wore a white linen napkin around his neck so as not to dirty his snow-white cravat. He spooned his stew into his mouth carefully. "This stew is excellent, Luanne," he told Ma.

I sat across from Gabe. Under the table he kicked my black, laced-up boot.

I giggled and lowered my head over my plate.

Immediately Pa saw something. "You two, behave yourselves. I've got Granville and Amelia at each other's throats and you two giggling like two geese at a pond full of fish. The only one who's behaving is Sis Goose. Now all of you behave or you can leave the table. Luanne, I've never tasted such wonderful stew."

This time I kicked Gabe's boot. He cleared his throat. I giggled and choked on a piece of bread.

Pa scowled. "Luli, you want to be spanked?"

"No, sir."

Pa threatened but he never acted on it with me.

Sis Goose gave me a very superior look because she knew I was up to something with Gabe and she was jealous she wasn't in on it. But she was comforted because she knew I'd soon be in trouble.

"You tell Old Pepper Apron she's outdone herself this time," Pa said.

"She didn't make it, she's ailing today," Ma told him. "I made it."

"Luanne." Pa put down his spoon and looked at her across the table. "After all these years, I never thought you could cook again like you used to."

Gabe couldn't take it anymore. He started laughing, and to hide it he covered his mouth with his white linen napkin and pretended he was choking.

"Drink some wine," Pa said. "Drink some wine, boy. For heaven's sake, it'll put hair on your chest, make you more handsome, the girls will be crazy over you. Give this family a good stew and they can't take it. Reminds me of the kind Edom would cook for me on the way to Mexico. Luanne, what's wrong with your children today?"

"I don't know," Mama said slowly. But she was looking at Gabe and then at me, slowly, knowingly, as if she *did* know, and I got scared. Still I started to laugh again until tears came to my eyes.

Pa slapped his hand down hard on the table. "Enough!"

I stopped. Gabe stopped.

"What in the name of the devil's purple ears is going on here with you two?"

"Sorry, sir," Gabe said. "I just had a choking fit."

Pa accepted that. "And you?" he asked me. "You just had a laughing fit?"

I knew when not to reply.

"You leave the table, little girl," he said. "Now. And take your muddle-headed brother with you. Both of you, out of my sight. Here we have solemn times. Fort Sumter's just been fired on by that fool Beauregard, South Carolina has seceded, and we're going to discuss this with our apple crisp and coffee for dessert. But you two won't be present. That's your punishment."

We didn't laugh, leaving. I'll say that for us. We didn't laugh until we got into the hall. Pa didn't understand. Both boys would soon be gone for soldiers. There was little time left for laughing.

CHAPTER SIX

WITH SIS GOOSE though, there was always time for laughing. She and I, growing up, were always in some mischief together. You would think, being nearly three years older than I, that she would have more common sense. She did when it suited her. But most of the time it didn't.

The only time it did was when she and Gabe became smitten with each other. Then those three years she had on me seemed like a hundred. She had entered a world that was a universe away from me and left me like a falling star, burning out, with a tail like tears trailing across the sky.

But that would come later when I would realize that what I had with Gabe was nothing compared to what she had with him. And that she had knowledge I did not have. That alone killed me.

When I was about ten, the year the war broke out, Sis Goose decided she wanted to know more about the birds and the bees. Young girls, of course, were supposed to be kept innocent. Ma was forthcoming with nothing except what we were to expect when we got our women's time of the month.

She didn't tell us why we got it. We were in total ignorance. It isn't as if we didn't associate with enough girls our own age to gossip about such things. We'd been to balls, hunts, horse races, taffy pulls, weddings, Christmas parties, and even corn huskings over the last year. But other girls our age didn't know any more than we did.

All were hungry for knowledge.

"You have to look in books," Lucy Raleigh of Peach Point Plantation wisely told us at a taffy pull.

When we got home, Sis Goose was after me to use Pa's library.

"It won't be in there," I told her.

"Then where?"

I thought a while. "Gabe's bookshelves," I said. "He's got all sorts of books. And he gave me permission to use them if I need to for my schoolwork. As long as I'm careful with them and put them back in place."

"What makes you think Gabe has a book like that?"

"Well, I don't know for sure. But Gabe knows everything. Where do you think he learned it?"

"Back in college."

Both boys were out of college now, working for Pa on the ranch, overseeing the men in the fields and the barns and corral, inspecting the care of the Thoroughbred horses. Sometimes riding out on the prairie to supervise the mending of fences. They left the house early in the morning and didn't come back until supper time.

Sis Goose took charge, as she was wont to do when she understood a situation. First she checked on the whereabouts of Ma and Pa and Amelia. Satisfied that they were out of the way, she led me quietly to Gabe's room and we sat on the Persian carpet next to his bed and beside his cherry bookcase.

I marveled at it. It spoke so much of Gabe, with the books lined up neatly and the book covers titled in gold writing.

The Raven by Edgar Allan Poe. He had a lot of Poe books. *The Vicar of Wakefield.* He had his collection of Charles Dickens, too. And *The History of Texas* and *The Conquest of Mexico* and so many others. There were schoolbooks on Latin and Greek, on science, trigonometry, and the study of the heavens, and Shakespeare, and so many others I cannot name them.

There were copies of *The Spectator* from when he visited Williamsburg and theater programs from that town and biographies of George Washington.

And then there was a book called *Rules of Civility and Decent Behavior,* which he'd told me about. George Washington had read it and abided by it.

"I've got it," Sis Goose said triumphantly. And she held up a pamphlet. "Imported from England." She showed me. "Oh, how wicked," she said.

In it were all the words and explanations we wanted to know.

We bent our heads over it together.

"Oh, look," she pointed, "there's the one I wanted to know. *Pimp.* Do you know what a pimp is?"

"No."

So she read it to me. And so I learned that afternoon, all the words that most young women from respectable families who were not married, and many who were married, did not know. "What does *ravished* mean?" I asked her.

"Well, here, read it; it's right here."

And so I learned another word. And I saw the pictures. And my face paled and I felt faint.

But in the next moment when I looked at Sis Goose, she started laughing. And I started, too, and soon we were both helplessly laughing and rolling on the floor. And the more we thought about it, the funnier it seemed.

"Do Ma and Pa do this?" I asked her.

"How do you think you all were born?"

I thought of Pa, stern, strict Pa, and I started another laughing fit. "Oh, oh, please," I begged her, "put the pamphlet back before I wet my pants."

She secured it in back of some books on the shelf where she'd found it. "Naughty Gabe," she said, and I had another thought. "Oh, I won't be able to look at him at supper without bursting into laughter," I said.

"What about your pa?"

"Oh please, Sis, don't look at me at supper, please."

She didn't.

We did things together like that, all the while we were growing up. We stole cookies from the pantry and ate them in our room at night in the dark. We told each other ghost stories in my bed, with the sheets over our heads, when we were supposed to be asleep. When the grown-ups were talking and laughing downstairs in the back parlor and we were supposed to be abed, she showed me a place she had discovered on the floor in our room, under the rug, where a trapdoor opened and the floor underneath was so thin you could hear every word said downstairs distinctly. She had a knack for intrigue, which, she said, she got from her father, the ship's captain.

One day Sis Goose took me into Amelia's room and we did each other's faces over with the face and lip rouge Amelia sometimes wore when her beau took her out. I can't imagine what Ma would do if she caught us. She was down in the quarters, helping to deliver a baby.

It was Gabe who caught us. He leaned against the doorjamb. "Well, you both look like tramps I've seen in New Orleans," he said.

We stood, stunned. We'd learned what a tramp was from Gabe's pamphlet. "You going to tell, Gabe?" Sis Goose asked.

"Tell who? Ma or Amelia?"

"Both."

"Love to tell Amelia. But no, I won't if you all take it off right now and promise not to do it again."

We promised. We kissed him. I wondered if he'd become friendly with the tramps in New Orleans.

WE WERE like sisters, Sis Goose and I, but we couldn't trade clothes because she was older and because she became a woman first. And then, at social gatherings, she started attracting the attention of young men. She was almost white, with just a hint of honey color, as if she'd stayed in the sun too long, and her complexion enhanced her beauty, added something to the clothes she wore. All the young men wanted to dance with her at balls and weddings. Oh, they danced with me, too, but that was part of the social scene, to be polite.

Pa said it was up to Granville and Gabe to keep their eyes cast in our direction. They were always watchful of us at gatherings, of course, but there was one occasion where Gabe had to come to Sis Goose's defense.

It was at a dance held after a morning's hunt. Of course, the women didn't go on the hunt. We languished about and lingered over breakfast; we displayed our musical skills; we rode for three or four miles. The men returned and after a lavish dinner there was dancing. The musicians were playing a waltz. Brit Borden was about the only young man of the planters' class who couldn't hold his liquor, and it was a mortal sin for a young man not to be able to hold his liquor.

He was dancing with Sis Goose, who was fifteen and looking like an angel in her blue gown with a hoopskirt.

I was dancing with Rutherford Burnet, who was sixteen and dying to go for a soldier, as my brothers had done. Both my brothers were home on leave, both dancing, both wearing their uniforms. But when the music ended, Brit wouldn't let Sis Goose go.

He held her and, right before everyone on the dance floor, kissed her. It all happened so fast. Gabe released his dancing partner and strode across the floor and grabbed Brit by the shoulder and dragged him from the room, past the glass doors and onto the lawn, where he commenced to whip him good.

"Leave my sister alone," I heard him saying. "You touch her again and I'll kill you."

Ma and Pa were watching. So was a tearful Sis Goose. Ma held her, with an arm around her shoulder. Pa said nothing. Just nodded his head in quiet approval.

From the ground, Brit spoke between spitting out blood. "She's not your sister, not the way I've seen you looking at her tonight, Holcomb. Why don't you admit it?"

It was the last thing he said before passing out. Granville had to pull Gabe off him. Never have I seen Gabe so angry. Oh, he didn't come away unscathed. He had a cut on his forehead and his knuckles were all bloody. And his lip was swollen. Later we found out, too, that he had a fractured rib. Granville had to bind it up.

But something happened that night. Lines were drawn across the starlit sky. Gabe's namesake, the angel Gabriel, blew his horn. I heard it inside me.

After that, Gabe started to treat Sis Goose differently. While he'd pull my hair or tweak my nose or still sit me on his lap, he regarded Sis Goose like a porcelain doll that might break. He'd nod and smile at her. Compliment her with as few words as possible, like "Pretty dress" or "Did you make this cake? Best I ever had."

I'd catch him staring at her when she wasn't looking. And I got scared.

When he left to go back to his post, all dressed up in his captain's uniform, he pulled me aside. "Take care of her."

"Well, I can't beat up Brit Borden like you did."

"He won't come within a mile of her, don't worry. Just . . ." and he closed his eyes and drew in his breath, "take care of her."

I could have teased him. But he looked so miserable I took pity on him. "I will," I said.

He nodded his thanks and kissed my forehead. "Good girl," he said.

I felt like one of his puppy dogs. And I knew, next to Sis Goose, that's how I'd feel from here on in.

CHAPTER SEVEN

ONE OF the things I dread most in my life is having to go and visit Aunt Sophie with Sis Goose. But one of the best things to come out of it is that, about a week before I go, Pa invites me into his study for a talk.

Now, if I've made Pa sound like a groundhog hibernating in his room, I've done him a disservice. He does come downstairs when the sky is blue enough, as he says, and attends to things in his study or even down at the quarters.

For any of us to be summoned before Pa is a privilege. We seldom are in his company, except at supper on a "blue-sky day." And then Amelia and I have to wear our best, copying Mama. And the boys, even if just in from the barn, must be freshly shaven and wearing their whitest of shirts and good jackets and shined boots.

Pa will not allow any troublesome matter to be discussed at supper. If matters are troublesome, he takes them, with Granville and Gabe, into his study after the meal is finished.

So to be invited into his study is special. Pa doesn't waste words.

Even my brothers feel like this. Although sometimes for them to be invited into Pa's study means they have done something to arouse his ire. Or I have, and he is holding them responsible.

Pa has a few iron rules for his sons. One is no dueling. The practice is outdated, yes, but there still is an occasional duel in Texas.

Another is to reverence Mama and their sisters and, indeed, all women. Which means they must never go to the quarters for their pleasure with women.

Pa is hard on the boys. Nevertheless, Gabe always tells me: "Listen to him, he's been around a long time. His advice is valuable. And don't ever sass him or you'll hear from me."

Now this visit to Pa's study was in preparation for my just-before-Christmas visit to Aunt Sophie's with Sis Goose. As if the matter had not been discussed and beaten to death already by Amelia and my brothers.

"You're a diplomat," Gabe told me about the visit, before he left to go back to Fort Belknap. "It's up to you to keep things even between Aunt Sophie and us, or we'll lose Sis Goose."

He stood before me. "That's what I'm supposed to tell you. What I *am* telling you is to remember that Aunt Sophie is a vulture in a hoopskirt. A black buffalo pawing the ground and getting ready to attack me. Remember that."

"Mama says she's planning a trip to England and wants to take Sis Goose along."

Gabriel gripped my arm then. "Don't let her, Luli. We can't allow that to happen. Say Sis Goose is sickly."

"But that would be lying."

His brown eyes bored into mine. "Then lie," he said.

I KNEW THAT Pa's ire was aroused by the subject of Aunt Sophie, too. Pa was too independent to allow a woman to push him around. Still, he respected the fact that in all legality Aunt Sophie *owned* Sis Goose, even though all the slaves were really free. Like the man in the barn had tried to tell us. Like we already knew.

"I'd try to convince her to free the girl, except that free negroes are considered a threat in Texas," he said to me once. "She'd be in more danger than she is now."

I never really thought of Sis Goose as being in danger. But she was, it seemed, no matter which way she turned.

"So this will be the Christmas visit then, hey?" Pa had asked me.

"Yes, sir," I said.

I got the impression that he was a little uncomfortable around me lately.

"You're growing up," he said, and it was almost an accusation.

"Yes, sir." I called him "sir" because the boys did. And

because it was Southern tradition. I don't know what Amelia called him and I didn't care.

Amelia was his pet, his first little girl, and he doted on her. The fact that I was a girl mattered, yes. But he seemed to expect more from me than from Amelia. It was as if he did not want the second girl to be a pet but a responsible woman.

"No more romping in the hayloft with Sis Goose, is it?" His eyes went over me. I was wearing my best calico and my boots were shined to perfection. Pa liked perfection.

"No, sir, we don't do that anymore."

He scowled. "You don't let that woman and her husband treat Sis Goose like a no-account servant," he said to me. "You know what I mean by that."

"Yes, sir."

"She's nothing but a grungy Comanche in disguise."

"Yes, sir." Inside I was laughing. I was pulling up weeds and throwing stones.

"If they try, you have my permission to take the girl and go out into the stable and get your horses and come home. It's a day's trip. You can do it. Take your gun."

"Yes, Pa, I will."

He looked at me again, studying on me, trying to figure out just what kind of a person I was. And was I up to his standards. Pa had high standards.

"Good then. You know what I want. If Gabe were here he'd take you and fetch you home. But he's off fighting

Indians again. Damned rascals won't stay put and mind the rules. I have no patience with anyone who won't mind the rules."

"Yes, Pa."

"As it is, your mother has made arrangements to have someone meet you at Shelby's Corners and escort you from there."

"Who?"

"All in good time. She'll tell you. Off with you now. Go on."

I was standing there stupidly, waiting. For what? I knew for what. For him to extend an arm and offer to enfold me to him. Sometimes he would do that. But not always. It depended on the mood he was in.

I curtsied and he nodded his head in approval. Then I left him there with his books and his accounts and his newspapers. Maybe he'd come out for supper this night and maybe not. I hoped the sky would stay blue enough.

WITH MAMA, I know she loved all her children, and that included Sis Goose. But somehow I always got the feeling that she favored the boys. "My boys," she'd call them, and she doted on them, worried for them, and still scolded them when the occasion warranted it.

The boys, so much taller than she was, took it all good-naturedly and teased and praised her on occasion. I know they loved her, but this isn't anything a man discusses with anyone: how he loves his mother.

I do know that she had a great influence on their lives and that they would go to her before going to Pa to ask for something. Sometimes she sent them straight to Pa. Other times she granted their wishes herself, wanting to spare Pa from some insignificant concern. I know the boys told her about the black man in the barn and how they sent him on his way. I don't think Pa ever knew about that.

After my audience with Pa, I was called to Ma. She had gestured that Sis Goose and I sit down at the kitchen table and have a cup of coffee before we left.

Ma had her own supply of real coffee beans that Granville had brought home for her after one of his running-the-blockade trips. She never asked him how he got it. She didn't want to know. But she saved it for special occasions.

Hot coffee! How good it smelled! "I think this is what we're really fighting the war for," I said jokingly. "And not the slaves."

Quickly I knew I'd said the wrong thing. From where Ma stood in the corner of the kitchen, peering into a butter churn at the fresh cream Molly, the servant, was going to churn, Ma gave me a look that would turn the cream sour.

She scowled and gestured with her head to Molly.

Not to Sis Goose, I minded. But Molly.

Mama didn't consider Sis Goose a slave. And she wouldn't stand for any claptrap from anybody who did.

That look demanded an apology, I knew. But to whom? I just lowered my eyes. "Sorry, Mama," I said.

"It's that kind of thoughtless talk that's going to get

you in trouble with Aunt Sophie," she said. "And then she'll accuse me of raising a little hoyden. And I do so want you girls to make a good impression on this visit. She's entertaining a very special guest."

Aunt Sophie always had special guests. She had turned their plantation, Glen Eden, into a social mecca. "You'd think she was Mrs. Lincoln," Pa had once said.

"Who's she entertaining this time?" I asked.

"Rooney Lee." Mama came over to the table and sat down opposite us, and I poured her a cup of coffee.

"General Lee's second son," she explained. "He rides with Major General Jeb Stuart. He's recovering from a leg wound he got at Brandy Station. Uncle Garland knows the Lee family and invited him to Glen Eden to recuperate."

My eyes were wide with wonder. "What is his rank?"

"Major general," Mama said. "Be kind to him, you two. He's lost two infants and his wife. And he's recently been a Federal prisoner. For nine months. He was just released eight months ago."

"Don't you remember?" Sis Goose said. "Mr. Porter told us all about the Lee family."

Mr. Porter was our tutor. He was away now for the winter break.

"Still, a real live major general. We'll get to talk to him, Sis. And find out what the war is about."

Mama sipped her coffee. "Why don't you just ask your brothers," she said dryly. Then she got up. Mama could not suffer fools gladly, and when I acted like one she was disappointed in me. Like Pa, she wanted to make me a strong, right-thinking woman. She tolerated no nonsense about boys, no unnecessary infatuation with clothes. The last thing in the world that she wanted me to be was a southern belle.

She herself had never had the chance to be one. Coming from the same plantation in Virginia as Aunt Sophie, she hated her sister's southern-belle ways and was determined to lead a useful life. And she had. She had worked hard with Pa to make our ranch successful. "A true man wants a partner," she'd told me once. "Not a gussied-up doll without a thought in her head."

Without her ever saying it, I knew she was disappointed in Amelia, who was a genuine southern belle. And she'd made up her mind she would succeed with me. So she let me ride astride, allowed Gabe to make me the best shot in the county (after him and Granville). She allowed me to clean my own gun and saddle my own horse and, since I was a toddler, to pad around after my brothers.

"Now," she said, "Major General Lee is riding out this day to meet you girls a quarter of the way to Glen Eden. He'll be waiting for you as soon as you get to Shelby's Corners. Remember, he is an honorable man from an honorable family. Make a good impression. And don't stare at his right hand. The tips of his fingers are missing."

"From what?" we both asked.

She smoothed down her white apron, without which she would not be seen during the day. She adjusted the kerchief at her neck and patted her brown hair in place.

"From when he was eight years old and went into the stable alone, disobeying his father. A horse bit them off. Come on now, it's time. Finish that coffee. Don't waste it."

We both gulped the rest of our coffee.

Mama held me, both hands on my shoulders, an arm's length away. "You'll do," she said. "Remember to offer to play the piano, and don't get puffed up about it. If Major Lee asks you to dance, remember yourself. And be gentle in his company. Don't ask questions of him. Just listen. Sometimes a man just needs to be listened to."

"Yes, ma'am."

"Do you have the homemade jellies and embroidered cloth I'm sending along?"

"It's all in my saddlebags, Ma."

She held me and kissed me. I could feel her heart beating. And I thought that God was good to me to give me such a mama.

Then she did the same to Sis Goose. And for the first time I didn't envy Sis Goose her looks. After all, her mama had died on a steamboat and she'd been handed over to people like a bale of cotton.

We set off. With some good riding we'd be at Shelby's Corners in less than an hour.

CHAPTER EIGHT

"Miss Luanne Holcomb, I presume. I'm William Fitzhugh Lee, your humble servant. You can call me Rooney, like my sisters do."

He took off his gray hat and gave as courtly a bow as one could while sitting astride a silver stallion.

"I'm Luli," I said. "And this is my almost-sister, Rose Smith."

"People call me Sis Goose," she said.

I saw Rooney's eyes go over her for just a second as a man's eyes go over a woman to take her measure. Then he put his hat back on his head. "And are you surviving as a goose in the courthouse full of foxes?" he asked pleasantly.

"Yes. No one has devoured me yet," she flung back.

I was glad to see that Rooney knew his Brer Fox and Brer Rabbit stories. It made this big, formidable-looking man, in his major general's uniform, less frightening. The uniform was the same tired gray as Gabe's, except that his looked as if he didn't have a woman to look after it. I'd given Gabe's a good brushing off many a time. And had one of the house servants press it.

We brought our horses up to his and set out together down the road to Glen Eden. "Who would call a pretty thing like you Sis Goose?" Rooney asked.

"My father," she replied.

"Ah yes, fathers tend to do that. My elder brother is named George Washington Custis Lee. More of a title than a name. Pa always called him 'Boo.' My father nicknamed me Rooney. I've heard, from your aunt Sophie, Sis, of the exploits of your steamboat-captain father. Well, I'm sure he means you to be a survivor. I see you two ride astride and not sidesaddle."

"My brothers insisted on it, Mister Rooney," I told him.

He laughed. "You'd be run out of town on a rail where I come from in Virginia. I know all about your brothers. Met Gabriel once. I almost talked him into riding with Jeb Stuart, but he said no. As for sisters, I have four. You remind me of my sister Mary. She's always been the rebel in the family. Moving out and spending her time elsewhere while my other two sisters care for my sick mama."

He talked a terrible lot for a man. But I sensed it was because he was nervous. Nervous? I smiled to myself. Unhorsed and rendered unconscious at South Mountain. Shot in the leg at Brandy Station. "I thought you had four sisters," I said.

He grew sober. "We lost Annie to typhoid near two years ago now."

"Oh, I'm so sorry." I was. This was precisely what

Mama hadn't wanted from me. What she meant when she said, "Be kind to him."

"My sister Annie gave my parents a run for their money, too. Blinded herself in one eye with a scissor when she was just six. As for Boo, Pa came upon him in camp one time when he had no coat but a Yankee one. He was in rags. Pa had to rustle clothing up for him. Yes, sir, I'm afraid we've, none of us, been easy for our parents."

"I think you have a wonderful family, Mister Rooney. Everyone reverences your father as a great man."

He drew in his horse and we did likewise. "I'm not in any rush to get back to Glen Eden. Your Uncle Garland has a slave trader visiting this day."

And he looked at Sis Goose. Then at me. "May I be candid?"

"Yes," I said.

He took off his gloves, and I saw the bitten-off fingers on his right hand. He ran that hand through his beard. "If I were in your shoes, Miss Rose, I'd plead a headache when I got there. No one thinks more of your aunt and uncle, but I'd make any excuse not to appear for supper. The slave trader will be at the table."

"Why's he here when his market will soon be gone?" I asked. Then realized I'd raised the wrong question in front of Sis Goose. The market was already gone, but I had to soften it, wrap it in the end of the war.

Rooney Lee sighed and plucked at his beard. "He has dear friends who could never have a child. They want a daughter and a companion. They're willing to put out money to buy one beautiful and accomplished and one they can educate in the best schools and make part of the family. The slave trader remembered Sis Goose from a past visit."

We all fell silent for a minute. Birds went from branch to branch in the trees above us, doing whatever it was they had to do to make a home. Rooney Lee picked up his reins and pressed his legs into his horse's sides. "Now let's get back," he said. And as I rode beside him I thought I heard him cuss under his breath, and say, "Ugly business."

But it was all too late, the warning. When we rode up the road and dismounted our horses and watched the stable boys take them away, I saw that the slave trader was right there on the front piazza with Uncle Garland and Aunt Sophie, sipping late-afternoon drinks.

"I'll handle this," Rooney Lee whispered to me. "Go and pay your respects."

We went up the few stairs to where they were sitting. "Well, it's about time," Uncle Garland said, getting out of his chair. "Jim," and he turned to the short, fat, balding man with the face and eyes of a ferret, "this is my niece Luli and the girl I was telling you about. Her name is Sis Goose. I told you she was a beauty, didn't I?"

I curtsied, but it went unnoticed by the ferret. He had eyes only for Sis Goose, and they went over her as one would appraise a horse. I expected, at any moment, that he would ask her to open her mouth so he could see her teeth or do some other horrid thing.

I hugged Aunt Sophie and so did Sis Goose.

"What household duties can she perform?" the slave trader asked.

At that moment Rooney Lee stepped forward. "The girl isn't feeling well, ma'am. I told her that you would excuse her from supper, knowing your capacity for understanding and sympathy."

Aunt Sophie immediately called a servant and had her take Sis Goose to her room upstairs. I was left standing there with Rooney Lee, son of the man who commanded the whole Southern army, just a little behind me.

I hadn't counted on Rooney's abilities to be both firm and gracious.

"The girl is the most beautiful piece I've ever seen," the slave trader said. "I wish you'd change your mind about selling her, ma'am. She could bring at least five thousand on the open market."

I felt faint. Apparently they'd discussed the matter beforehand, and Sis Goose and I had walked into a trap.

"It is my understanding that the young lady is family," Rooney said.

And he looked at me for confirmation. So I answered, "She is. You know how my mother feels about her, Aunt Sophie."

"But I've never had the chance to enjoy her as family. And she belongs, by rights, to me, and not your mother."

"Here," Rooney said. And he took my hand. "We're all tired. Of course she belongs to you, ma'am. If you allow me to take Luli here for a walk, I'll soothe things down."

My head was spinning. I was here five minutes, yet in that time everything was spilled out all around us. Like blood.

I went with Rooney for a walk through the English gardens.

ONCE WE were out of earshot he stopped walking and looked at me. "Excuse me for being nosy, but does she know she's already free?"

The question was blunt. He was no longer being polite. "No," I said.

"You haven't, as her friend, told her?"

"My brothers warned me not to. Granville says we're not part of the states. And if the rumor takes on legs and starts running, there might be a slave uprising in Texas."

"How selfish we are," he mused. "I was never so amazed as when I first came here to see that the slaves don't even know about Lincoln's proclamation."

"We don't get much intelligence from back in the states."

"No. You're like a different world out here. Of course none of us in our family really believed in the institution of slavery. My pa is fighting to win the war, but he himself believes there should be no north, no south, no east, and no west. Just America, the Union. He sees bondage as a moral and political evil."

He paused for a minute.

"Will you tell any of the slaves here that they should be free?" I asked.

He smiled. "I'm wined and dined here. I know I represent my pa. So no, I won't let the cat out of the bag. I've no interest in being hanged. And speaking of cats, and to give the conversation a new turn, do you want to hear about my father's cat back at Arlington?"

"Of course."

"We were forced to leave Arlington House and abandon it to the Yankees. My mama was brokenhearted. We left most of the furnishings and Tom, my pa's cat. Tom and Pa got on famously. Pa misses him powerful much. And he hopes Tom lords it over those Yankees and, as host, ignores them, too."

I laughed. I was meant to laugh. He wanted to strike a lighter note. We started walking back to the house where the candlelight and music seemed so welcoming.

By the time I left Glen Eden, I was in love with Rooney Lee. Not in a southern-belle way, but in a way that recognized all the pain in him. The sorrow. I never saw him again after that week. But I did not forget the big solemn man who had lost so much besides the war.

CHAPTER NINE

ON THE third day of that visit, Uncle Garland left with Rooney Lee for a fox hunt and a stay at a nearby plantation. Aunt Sophie had declined to go. She had other fish to fry, she told her husband, and it turned out that she did.

For some reason she determined that it was time to train Sis Goose in some household arts. To make her "more valuable as a personal maid."

She did not tell the menfolk her plans. I suspect she knew that Rooney Lee would not approve. So as soon as they were gone she called the two of us before her.

"Luli, for the next two days find yourself something to do. I see you have brought your embroidery, and you may take advantage of your uncle's library if you wish. I am going to be busy with Sis Goose."

And without missing a beat she turned to Sis Goose, who was standing beside me. "You come upstairs with me. This day you are going to learn how to dress a lady's hair. Then you will go to the kitchen and find out just how I want my eggnog done. And if you do well, tomorrow you'll learn how I want my clothes in the clothes press, how to care for them, and how to make candied violets."

I heard Sis Goose gasp. "Ma'am, nobody told me this."

"Well, I'm telling you now."

"At home I don't, that is, I never had to do more than take Mr. Holcomb's morning coffee into the study. And I considered that a privilege."

Good for you, I thought. *You sound just right. Sure of yourself, yet no sass.*

Myself, I asked, "To what end is all this learning of household chores?"

"Household arts," Aunt Sophie corrected.

She'd already started for the stairway, Sis Goose in tow. "Must I tell you, like I had to tell your brother? Didn't you hear Mr. Dodd ask me what Sis Goose was trained up for? A good ladies' maid, a practiced household girl, is highly prized."

Mr. Dodd, the slave trader, had thankfully left that same night. I could not keep silent. "You mean you aim to sell her," I said.

"The truth is, she is trained up for nothing," Aunt Sophie went on. "And if, God forbid, something happened to me or my husband, Sis Goose would be sold as part of the estate. If there is a recession, we might have to sell her.

And with this war nobody knows what will happen. What is she good for? Tell me."

"The war is almost over, Aunt Sophie," I said, "and so is everything that goes with it."

"You hush your mouth now, girl. Don't you know enough to hush your mouth?"

"She's my sister. I don't aim to hush up about that. She's beautiful and sweet and my parents love her. She's my friend."

I was starting to anger her. "If you aren't as danged irritating as that Gabriel brother of yours. She's listed, in my farm book, as one of the slaves, loaned out to your parents," she went on. "And since she can't do any household tasks, she'd be sold off and her new owner would put her in the fields. And even if the slaves are freed with the end of the war, she'd be left wandering loose, with nothing to do. You and your mother and brother are living in a fairy tale, Luli. I'm doing this not to demean her but to protect her."

"My parents wouldn't let her wander loose." I don't know where I got the gumption, but I said it.

She did not get angry. She just gave out a big sigh because both of us hit that brick wall again.

I felt bad discussing Sis Goose as if she weren't there, like she was a commodity and not a person. I just blinked through tears that were gathering in my eyes. And watched them go up the stairs.

"I'm coming, too," I called up.

"Suit yourself," Aunt Sophie said. "But if you distract her, I'll ask you to leave."

THERE WAS nothing for me to do but sit there while Sis Goose obediently draped a white cloth around Aunt Sophie's shoulders and took up a brush to have a go at her hair.

From time to time Aunt Sophie would direct. "Harder. Not that hard. I don't need to be scalped. There, now you've got it right."

"Let me try," I said, getting up.

Aunt Sophie sighed but allowed me to have a go at her half-brown, half-gray hair. I pretended to be enjoying it and smiled at Sis Goose as if it were all a game.

If she must do it, then so would I, I decided. That way Sis Goose wouldn't feel demeaned.

The hair was then braided and the braids curled up on top of her head. Then two wisps of hair must be curled down on the side of each ear. Sis Goose learned to use a curling iron that morning, burning herself twice. At home neither of us went through this with our hair. She wore hers straight down her back or in a single braid. I had natural curls and had all I could do to control them.

Finally the operation was over. While it had been going on, Safron, who was Aunt Sophie's personal maid, had been making the bed and fussing about the room. As she was about to pick up the chamber pot to take it downstairs and empty it, Aunt Sophie got inspired.

"Leave that, Safron. Sis Goose will tend to it."

Immediately a bell went off in my head and I felt for a minute as if Gabriel were standing there beside us. But it was my father's voice that I heard.

If she treats Sis Goose like a no-account, you have my permission to take your horses and leave.

"No," I said. And I stepped forward. Safron stopped. Everyone did, it seemed. Aunt Sophie was patting her hair and peering at herself in the mirror. But she stopped cold, too.

"What is the meaning of this? How dare you revoke my orders? Sis Goose, take up the pot."

Sis Goose stood unmoving, confused. I stepped between the pot and her. "She isn't here to empty chamber pots," I said firmly.

"It's part of her job."

"She doesn't have a job. If you make her do it, we will leave."

She sneered. "And say what to your mother when you get home?"

"Pa said we could. He said if you treat Sis Goose like a no-account, we should get our horses and leave."

She didn't expect that. She'd had many an argument with Mama, but she was a little afraid of my pa. He took no sass from her.

"If you do that," she said evenly, "I shall exercise my rights and take her back. And there's nothing you or your pa or your precious brothers can do about it."

Sis Goose stepped in then, bless her. "No disrespect, ma'am, but if you make me live here, I'll run away."

"And be caught by the first slave catcher roaming the countryside. They're still out catching runaways, you know. And you'd be sold into slavery. And I swear, I will not stop it."

We were deadlocked, stuck in the mud like pigs after a hard rain. And then I had a thought.

"She can do all the chores she wants," I conceded, "except the chamber pot. If you make her do that, I'll tell Rooney Lee when they get back. I'll bring it up at supper."

Aunt Sophie blinked and her cheeks flushed. She did not want to be known amongst the cream of Southern society as a cruel and nasty woman. She did not want censure from Rooney Lee. What if he told his father?

I had her where I wanted her. Like a fox in a leg trap.

"Very well then," she said, "no chamber pot. Safron, you may take it out. But there will be other chores. Does making candied violets suit you?"

"You should know that we're, neither of us, strangers to the kitchen," I told her quietly. "Mama wouldn't allow that. I can fry bacon and make a decent pecan pie. So can Sis Goose. My brothers are mad for my sugar cookies. I can not only shoot a wild turkey but bring it home, strip off the feathers, take out the innards, and cook it. And Sis Goose makes a rhubarb pie that the Yankees would lay their guns down for. But no," I allowed, "we've never made candied violets. And we'd both like to."

CHAPTER TEN

FIRST WE had to dip the violets, which Aunt Sophie had dried and preserved, into beaten egg whites. Then we held each violet upside down by the stem and dipped it carefully into sugar until they were coated. Then we set them aside, one by one, to dry and be stored away.

Suzy, the kitchen maid, showed us how. I'll say one thing for Aunt Sophie: She knew which flowers you could eat and not become sick from. She always served some kind of flowers at her table.

"In Europe they do this," she told us.

I could have told her that you didn't have to go to Europe to eat flowers. Mercy Love, our own hoodoo woman at home, ate them all the time.

We enjoyed making the candied violets that day. And afterwards we rode out into the brisk December air to cut and bring home holly and evergreen branches. Tomorrow, when the men got home, we were going to help Rooney Lee and the servants decorate the house.

The next few weeks before Christmas there would be

a round of visiting on the plantations. My parents would start theirs off by coming here and fetching us home.

We all hoped the boys would make it home for the holidays. Gabe always rode out and cut the tree, and Granville brought home the big yule log.

After the candied violet episode, Aunt Sophie becalmed herself a little and entered into the spirit of the season. After all, she must supervise the blowing up of hog bladders for children to pop over the fires; there were her slaves who would sing for her company and they had to be practiced; not to mention baking to be done, turkeys to be readied, and dances to be planned.

WE WENT home with Ma and Pa after two days to keep our own Christmas. And so Sis Goose and I had to ride out again to get the holly and evergreens. We popped the corn to string on the tree, the tree that Sam the overseer brought in because Gabe never made it home in time. Part of that holiday included the visit Sis Goose and I paid to the hoodoo woman.

Every Christmas season it was our job to bring Mercy Love her gifts. Pa picked out what she was to have because all year long she kept him apprised of what the weather would be. Several times a year, when the sky was blue, he'd take up his cane and put on his best frock coat and cravat and walk down to the quarters to visit Mercy Love. Sometimes Sis Goose and I would go with him, one on each side, holding his arms. But we'd wait outside the small log cabin, if we went along, for him to come out.

"Rain," she'd tell him. "Lots of rain. The moon is tilted downward so the water can come out."

"In how many days?" Pa would ask. And she'd answer, "Count the number of stars in the halo around the moon."

She was always right, Pa said. You could set your clock by her predictions, whether they be about storms or drought. To a cotton and wheat and corn planter, this meant more than gold.

So Christmastime Sis Goose and I took her tokens of appreciation from Pa. Actually, he kept her supplied regular-like in shanks of ham and bacon and a possum or two for her pot, potatoes and sorghum, and even rum. She especially liked rum.

This year we took a ham bundled in burlap, a side of bacon, and a heap of sugar cookies. She ate like a ranch-hand, that woman, and she was the skinniest little bit of a thing.

She kept an owl in her cabin. Her husband had long since died and she said she buried him standing up and facing west, with his jug of corn likker at his feet.

I don't know where she got it, but when we visited she always had candy for us. Peppermint and wintergreen.

Her small log house was surrounded with hedgerows of Cherokee roses, an evergreen with the sharpest of thorns. No animal or human could get through unless you knew the place on the side where there was a break in the hedgerows and you could shimmy through sideways.

Of course she could see the future. That goes without saying. She did it with cards or with tea or by reading your palm. I got the feeling they were only props and it all just came inside her head.

This time it was still early in the day, but the darkness was already threatening. She had candles lighted all over her cabin. And seated on the table, right next to her, was Sasquatch. He peered at us with eyes as impenetrable as a backwoods swamp. He was a snowy owl. I'd looked him up in one of Pa's books. His Latin name was *Nyctea scandiaca.* And he was a rare bird that sometimes honored Texas with his appearance.

He ruffled his feathers and raised his wings, showing off his wingspan.

He would never fly again. He'd come to her with a broken wing, which she'd mended. But whether it was not mended right or he refused to leave her, she would never know.

"Like with some people," she told us, "it's better we don't know."

She wore something black that draped around her and she smiled at Sis Goose. "How you doin', little girl?"

"I'm fine, ma'am."

She would not take her eyes off Sis Goose. It was like I didn't exist.

Today she was reading tea leaves. And as she peered at them in the bottom of the cup she said to Sis Goose quietly, "You ready to meet your papa?"

Sis Goose smiled. "I haven't seen him since I was a knee baby. Why would I see him now?"

"Only he knows that. Maybe he come to fetch you home."

"I don't belong to him anymore. I belong to Aunt Sophie, remember?" Sis Goose asked.

Only then did Mercy Love look at me; a long, haunting look. And in that instant it was as if I could hear her speaking inside my head. "So, you ain't told her she's free yet, is that it?"

Then she broke into insane laughter. But there were tears in her eyes.

"This war be over soon," she said. "An' then you all be free."

"And you?" I dared ask it. "What will you do when you're free, Mercy Love?"

She shook her head and sighed. "I's free now, little girl. And when they say I am I won't ever be." More laughter. "You go on and figure that out."

She gave us gifts. She came forward with two pennies, each wrapped in tissue paper. "Put these in your left shoes," she ordered.

We each took off our left shoe and put the pennies in. "What will they do?" Sis Goose asked.

"Wear them for three days, then throw them in the

creek. Keep you from the cholera or the bilious fever or typhoid."

We dared not disbelieve her.

Then she brought to the table a bowl of clear water and some soap. "Wash your hands together," she said, "so you can be friends for life."

We did so, gladly. Then she gave us each a conjure bag, with goofer dust from the graveyard in it. For good luck.

As we turned to leave she patted my shoulder. "You should know that Gabriel brother of yours will be home soon," she said, "though he have a wound in his leg from the Indians."

Before I could say anything, she laughed. "But he ain't your Gabriel brother anymore. He's this one's lover." And she laughed quietly. Then, "You bring me a piece of his clothing," she said to Sis Goose, "an' I keep him safe for you."

I drew in my breath, wondering why, when the war was almost over, I had feelings that worse times were yet to come.

CHAPTER ELEVEN

Sis Goose's lover.

Sometimes Mercy Love teased. Most times likely not. The thing is you have to remember that that Christmas of '64, Sis Goose was sixteen already and I still a child of thirteen. Sure, she sometimes acted younger than me. Sometimes Gabe told me to look after her when he was gone, and I did. But when it came to falling in love, when it came to Gabe, she was somehow looking like twenty.

There were days she wanted nothing to do with me because of the age difference, days she considered herself older than the stars and full of secrets I'd never be privy to. These days she'd hurt me and I'd secretly cry. And there were days she shared with me her dreams and some of those secrets and I needed nothing else to keep going.

The house was all decorated with garlands on the banisters and fruit on the mantels, and the tree in the parlor glowed with candles and smiled with cut-out paper decorations and strung popcorn and berries. With both my brothers home, the house took on another life, the way it did when there were men around. Their hound dogs lounged in front of the hearths, dirty paws and all. There wasn't much Ma could say about it. The dogs were usually confined to the front hall, but the boys loved them too much.

Mama said we were starting to look like a book by Charles Dickens. She looked at me in my ruffled skirts, my polished boots, my high lace-collared blouse, and my dark hair drawn back with a ribbon, when she said it.

"Go upstairs and get your brothers down, Luli," she said. "Mr. Smith and your pa haven't got all morning."

Mr. Smith was Sis Goose's father, the ship's captain, come to visit. A surprise visit, though Sis Goose and I had been forewarned by Mercy Love. He was in Pa's study, having a wake-up toddy and talking.

Sis Goose hadn't met him yet. She was just about champing at the bit, helping Ma see over last-minute details of the table.

I went upstairs, sneaked down the hall, and stood silently outside the door of Gabe's room.

"Mr. Gabriel, sir." It was Arnold, Granville's "man," who went everywhere in attendance with him. He was helping Gabe with his cravat. Gabe was an utter failure with that particular piece of menswear.

"I know she's there, Arnold," Gabe said, calmly adjusting what Arnold had done on the necktie. "You have to get used to her," he teased. "You'll find critters like her all over the house this time of year. Well, step out into the open, miss. Do you have something important to tell me?"

"Yes."

"I'm waiting."

It was about the lotion Granville had brought home from Mexico. He was wearing it. I was disappointed in him. He never used such rot.

"You smell like a pimp," I told him. "You go downstairs smelling like that and Pa will put you with the hogs."

He stopped fixing his cravat. He adjusted the suspenders on his shoulders. He looked like I'd thrown yesterday's hog slop in his face. "Where'd you learn that word?"

I shrugged. "I know just about as much as Sis Goose does about things."

"Do you now?"

"Uh-huh."

"Well then, you better know enough to run for your life right now, little girl. Because if I catch you, I'll take you right to Granville and you can tell him your opinion about the lotion he brought home. And we'll let him decide what to do with you. You know Granville's not very patient with little girls who bad-mouth their elders. Did you know that?"

My stomach was starting to churn. I shook my head no.

"Now, go on. Get the hell out of here."

He must have drank too much last night, I decided, or he'd never speak to me like that. That in itself was worse than anything Granville could do to me. I left.

TWENTY MINUTES later we were all seated around Mama's Christmas breakfast table, eating the specialties I and Sis Goose and Mama and the servants had prepared all week. Everything between Gabe and me had been forgotten, or so it seemed. Mr. Smith was still in Pa's study with him.

Pa had sent out word for us to go ahead and eat.

The boys were solemn on this visit, because the end of the war was in sight. And the South was bound to lose. Granville had brought the big-city newspapers, like gold to us, and they all said Atlanta, Georgia, had fallen in the autumn.

Ma comforted the boys. She said they'd fought the good fight and that was all that mattered. After all, the Yankees weren't here yet. We might still get a spring crop planted before they came and freed all the slaves.

I finished my breakfast and went to stand by Gabe, hoping to be forgiven and not sent away. These were serious matters they were discussing, and I needed comfort.

He took me on his lap as he told of rumors that certain groups of men were talking of running off in vigilante actions, to the west. Outriders, thieves, if necessary.

Mama said she didn't want to hear any talk about running off and joining a passel of rebels hiding in the hinterlands and holding out against the Yankees. That we had to get on with our lives, and if either Granville or Gabe did such a thing, she'd gather a group of ranch hands and come find them and whip them good.

Both my brothers smiled for the first time that morning.

"We have to figure out how we're going to run this place without slave labor," she said. "Some planters are talking about hiring Scottish laborers."

I loved listening to discussions like this, to the words that flew back and forth like doves between my family. I loved listening and learning. I leaned my head back on Gabe's chest, heard his heart, then heard something else.

"*Psst,* Luli, come here. Now."

The door to Pa's study was open just wide enough so Sis Goose and I could peek in without being seen.

"He's so tall," Sis Goose whispered of the man inside there with my pa.

"Yes. And handsome. Almost as handsome as Gabe."

"Why is he wearing a uniform?" she asked me.

"It's the uniform of a ship's captain," I told her. It was a wild guess, but the uniform was blue and I was sure he wasn't a Yankee.

"Luli, get away from that door." Gabe's voice floated down the hall from the dining room.

We didn't move right away. We continued peeking.

"Luli, you want me to come over there?"

If he did, what would he do? Pull me away and leave Sis Goose? Here was where it got sticky as spilled honey. She didn't have to obey him, but I did? All my life she'd been another little sister to him and now she wasn't anymore.

I backed off from the door. It was easier that way.

Just then Pa opened it, smiling, "Well, little lady? You ready to see your pa?"

"Yes, sir," Sis Goose said.

To my surprise Pa came out and gave them their privacy. I wanted to go in. I made a move toward it, but Pa grabbed my arm and said, "She can do this without you."

They were in there near an hour visiting. I went back to the table, pulled there by Gabe's look. When Sis Goose came out she was holding two packages wrapped in brown paper. Her eyes were glistening and she set the packages aside and sat down at the table with us.

"Is he going to take you away with him?" Gabe asked.

I hadn't thought of that. Only Gabe would. "No," she said shakily.

What if he wanted to? I wondered. What rights did Gabe have? Oh, I was so confused. Then before I knew it, Pa asked me to fix a dish of breakfast and bring it into the study for Captain Smith. He was busy with some papers. And although he'd brought us a large basket filled with wine, sugar in cones, coffee beans, and a giant ham, he didn't have time to join us, thank you.

The food, it turned out, was just an excuse. Mr. Smith wanted to see me.

"I understand you've been looking after my daughter all these years," he said to me.

He wore a beard that was part white, though he was not yet an elderly man. His blue eyes were piercing but unfathomable as the river currents he maneuvered every day. His blue coat was open and I could see that he wore a pistol, something long handled and carved.

"Some people would say she looks after me," I answered bravely.

He settled back in his chair and sipped his coffee. "I like you. You're straightforward. No duplicity about you." He smiled. "You haven't told Sis Goose yet that she is free, I hear."

This man doesn't waste time, I thought. "No."

"Good. I was just telling your pa that I'm glad of it. There's no telling what notion she'll get in her head if she knows it. I don't need her running off with some roustabout like her mother ran off with me."

I was shocked into silence.

"You keep on being her friend," Captain Smith went on. "She'll need one in the future."

"She's my sister," I said. "I can't think of her any other way."

He nodded approvingly. "Good girl. I've brought her a fine velvet cloak for Christmas. And one for you. You can wear them together and be sisters."

Then it was over, for me at least. Pa went back in his study for more conferring. "Likely they're talking about how to make money with the end of the war." Mama never glossed over things.

I don't know why, but I expected Gabe to meet with Sis Goose's father that day. Isn't that what you did with the father of your intended? Or wasn't he serious? Was it all one of Sis Goose's dreamed-up secrets?

I'd have to wait to find out.

THE GIFTS Sis Goose got from her pa were long cloaks of blue velvet trimmed with fur. "For the day when you come aboard ship," the note read.

For just a moment I envied her. You could see, if you were blind as a skunk in daylight, how happy she was. I just didn't know how much of it was from her pa's visit and how much because of Gabe.

We had Christmas. The slaves were given the week between Christmas and New Year's off, except for feeding the livestock, milking, and gathering eggs.

It was my job, with my brothers, to give the slaves their gifts on Christmas morning when they came up to the big house to stand outside by the front steps. I stood between my brothers and now Sis Goose stood with us.

Mama insisted we wear our long blue velvet coats. And I was surprised at how much it made us feel even closer, how we giggled and smiled as we handed out the gifts.

The children got candy and small sacks of pennies. The men and women each got a new blanket and a pair of shoes.

The tradition on our place was that the holiday lasted as long as the yule log burned, so the household help made sure that log kept burning all right.

In between the festivities, the visitors, the dancing,

Pa and Mama and the boys met frequently in Pa's study, talking about what was to come in this new year of 1865.

The war would end soon now. It was only a matter of months. The slaves would be freed. "We'll not tell them about the war's end until the spring planting is done," Pa said. "I know that's what Henry Ware of Oak Grove plans on doing."

I was in on that meeting for reasons I can't recollect. But not Sis Goose.

"How many of our people do you think will stay after they're told?" Mama asked.

"A goodly amount. We'll have to pay them, of course. But I can't hit home enough with the idea that *things must stay the same for as long as we can keep them that way,*" Pa said.

Yes, we all agreed. The same as always. Until always was not just a word but a family's history and livelihood.

Things must stay the same.

I THOUGHT Gabe forgot, but he didn't. He called it paying your debts. He called it Southern honor.

He brought me to Granville before that visit was over and made me tell him what I thought of the lotion he'd brought home, then left me there with him, in his room, alone.

Granville's room was filled with foreign remembrances,

pictures of ships (for, yes, we had photos now), awards for seamanship, and him.

He wasn't clean-shaven like Gabe. He had a beard, dark eyes, a slight but lithe build. I was afraid of him.

As it turned out, he didn't believe in making a child work herself to death in the barn as punishment, or copy some glorious section of the Bible, or iron his shirts for a week, or write up the history of his lotion, or even in spanking. But he did believe, oh how he believed, in washing the mouth out with vile-tasting soap, the kind the ranch hands used to wash up with. After all, that's where the dirty word had come from, didn't it? And wasn't that tradition? And mustn't things stay the same?

He took me outside, out back, where there was a trough to wash up in and where I afterward threw up.

Somehow I think Gabe knew what Granville did to me. Because I caught him looking at me once in a while across the table that night with that somber and sorrowful gaze.

Granville was quietly unsorry about it. It was done. *Don't make me have to do it again. And don't go running to Ma.*

I couldn't eat supper, so I didn't. "I don't feel so well, Ma. I'm kind of under the weather. I can't eat. Can I go lie down?"

She wouldn't excuse me. She knew, and she always

backed up the boys. So I sat there, green in the face and near tears.

Guilty as a deer eating Ma's daylilies, Gabe was, and wanting to make it up but not knowing how. If only I could keep him that way.

I WATCHED GABE and Sis Goose all the time now, when they didn't know I was watching. I saw that he had special looks for her and she for him, looks that did not require words. How could I have been so blind before, thinking nothing of it when he lifted her off her horse, or his hands lingered a little longer when he helped her on?

Sis Goose and I slept in the same room, so I kept my mouth shut when she came to bed later than usual after taking a walk with Gabe.

And, lying there in my bed, waiting for her to come up, my mind would race and whirl.

Would he tell her she was free?

Did she think, now, that he owned her so he had a right to love her? Would she marry him if she were not a slave?

When would he tell her? Was he afraid that if he told her beforehand, she'd "run off with some roustabout," as her father had said?

What would she say? "I can't forgive you for keeping me in bondage. I can't marry you, Gabe."

"Take care of her," Gabe admonished me when his holiday furlough was over and he left for Fort Belknap.

If he didn't have to wait for the circuit preacher to come through, would he have wed her before he left? I recollected how antsy my sister got waiting for that preacher before she married in December of 1863.

Now it would be at least two months until Gabe came home again. If he could get away. And who knew when, after that.

As IT TURNED out, it was March when he again came home. The end was coming. Soon General Lee's line at the James River at Petersburg and Richmond would have to be abandoned.

"He doesn't have enough troops to hold off Sherman in the Carolinas," Gabe told us. "I've asked to be sent to help, but it turns out our frontier here would be abandoned to the Indians, and I'm afraid they don't care who wins the war. They just insist on being a threat."

Mama was distraught. She hugged him. Who was worse, she tried to decide, the Kickapoos or the Yankees?

With Gabe home, Sis Goose once again was coming up to the room long after I had gone to bed. I would lie there waiting for her, wondering just when it was that things had changed between her and Gabe. And what would become of it.

The night before he left again for Fort Belknap, Sis Goose came in especially late. Actually, it was near morning. Where had they been?

Late the next morning, Gabe saddled up and bid

good-bye to us all, telling me to take care of Sis Goose, who stood to the side with tears in her eyes.

That afternoon I went, as I did most days, to take a plate of supper to Edom in the log house that Grandpa had built.

"Nice warm fire," he said, stoking it with a poker. "Burned all night long. He kept it burning."

"Who?" I asked. But I knew instantly, even before he answered.

"That young brother of yourn. Gabe. In here with that woman of his near the whole night."

So. This is where they had stayed. How stupid of me. Of course. All the privacy they wanted here. Edom slept in the back room.

GABE WAS back at Fort Belknap when the war ended. We kept the ending from the slaves as well as we could.

The vegetable and flower gardens were planted. All the fences were mended. Fertilizer was put in the fields. But it wasn't enough.

The cotton must be planted. So must the wheat and corn.

All the slaves were set to work. Pa, usually a wonderful host, deliberately cut off contact with anyone on the outside. He wanted no news of war's end, no hint of freedom to reach our slaves until he absolutely had to tell them.

Was it right? We didn't discuss it. Did they suspect? They had no outside information, not even in the slave grapevine, because Pa forbade the visiting back and forth to other plantations, even by men or women who had wives or husbands there. And they had Sam the overseer's cooperation.

We became a country unto ourselves. *Did it matter?* we asked ourselves. *Who would be hurt with a couple of more months in bondage?*

I am sure God has that question written down in a dark book in gold print somewhere.

CHAPTER TWELVE

PA HEARD, through his own connections, which he did not even tell Mama about and which she didn't ask him, that the Yankees were finally coming in June.

We think he had something to do with the commission of men sent to New Orleans by Governor Pendleton Murrah to make peace terms with the Yankees.

The men asked if the slaves could remain on their plantations until the crops were gathered. The Yankee officials said no.

On June 19, 1865, General Gordon Granger issued the Emancipation Proclamation for Texas. Exactly two years and five months after the slaves back in the states heard of it.

"Sir." Sam the overseer, faithful to Pa up until then, came to the big house to see him. "Sir, I can't hold out no longer. They's bound to find out and if'n you doan tell 'em soon, I'm afeared they'll all walk off from you. If'n you do tell 'em and ask nice, I think you got a good chance of havin' many of 'em stay. With some agreement, of course."

Pa trusted Sam and agreed. And so he stayed locked in

his study all day and would take no vittles. Nor would he answer the knocks on the door. Mama finally got Sis Goose, whom I suspected he favored as much as me, to knock on the door and call in, "Mister Holcomb, sir? I have your coffee. Just the way you like it. And some ham and biscuits."

Maybe he was just starved. Maybe he'd lost track of time, drawing up the freedom order to be read to the slaves. He let Sis Goose in. And he kept her with him the whole afternoon, asking her how the order read, sounding it off her. Then he said, "And where will you stand when the order is read, child?"

He knew what he was asking. "With my people, if you wish," she answered.

"Your people are us. Will you stand with us?"

"Yes, sir."

"Will you wear that blue cloak and stand beside my daughter when she wears hers?"

"It's warm for a cloak," she said.

"Just the same," he asked.

She could refuse him nothing. She said yes and repeated the conversation to me while we were dressing and putting on our twin blue cloaks. "He sees me as one of you," she said wonderingly.

"And why not? Aren't you practically wed to Gabe?"

She sobered.

"I know you spent the last night of his leave in March with him in the log house," I told her. "Edom told me."

She bit her lower lip. "There are some things I can't tell you, though you are my sister," she said. "Please understand that. There will always be secrets between Gabe and me."

I nodded. "Are there more, then?" I asked.

"I've told you all I can for now," she promised.

I believed her.

I AND MAMA and Sis Goose stood with Pa on the front steps of thc big house and all the slaves, summoned by Sam, came to stand in the drive below.

Pa read the freedom papers. Sis Goose held my hand, and I saw some of their eyes go over us in the identical blue coats. Mercy Love was one of these. Her eyes saw us standing there and her eyes saw all.

They knew Sis Goose, knew she lived in the house with us, was tutored with me, was indeed one of us. But they still seemed surprised that she was not standing with them.

I saw what Pa was doing, placing her with us, showing us as sisters. He was telling them how well she'd been treated, reminding them of how well he'd treated them all. Good food, adequate clothing, no whippings, care when they were sick, all of it. He hoped they'd remember.

Pa told them they were free. General Gorden Granger had said so. He had marched into Galveston yesterday, the nineteenth, to establish the sovereignty of the United

States and the Yankee troops marching into Texas over the defeated Confederates.

Our slaves drowned out his other words with their whoops and hollers and hugs. They jumped up and down. They danced, they held each other. They pulled up grass and threw stones, they yelled in the air, much the same as Grandpa Holcomb had done when he claimed his property.

"Hallelujah! Hallelujah!" they yelled. They knelt down on the ground and thanked the Lord. Finally they quieted down.

"I don't know what plans you have, but I see that some of you were prepared for this announcement," Pa said, pointing at old carpetbags and bundles of things some of them had at their feet. "I see some of you are planning to leave. But think. Where will you go? I have no more financial responsibility for you. But if you wish to stay on, if this place has become your home, and if you will agree to continue working for us, I'll continue to give you shelter, food, clothing, everything you've always had, plus either a share of the crops or a small wage. I'll bring in a tutor to educate you, so you can read and write. That's the best I can do for now."

Pa's voice broke. He turned to go into the house. Mercy Love raised a hand and gestured toward Pa.

I prayed she would say nothing about knowing they'd been free for over two years now. She didn't. "Bless you, sir," she yelled to Pa. "I's be stayin'."

A few others called out the same thing. They moved together, to the side, in one group. I noticed, thankfully, that Old Pepper Apron, the white-haired buxom cook, was one of them. "Nobody gettin' in my kitchen," she said.

A group of field hands moved forward and murmured that they would stay. "Leastways 'til the crops is in, boss," one said. And the others agreed in a chorus of "yeahs."

By the time Pa went through the front door, he was weeping.

The Yankees came two days later.

WE FIRST SAW them as if in a dream, Sis Goose and I. We had just returned from doing a tour of the ranch, something the boys did when they were home, to inform Pa if there were any fences down, any trees in need of tending, and even how the wild buffalo clover was in abundance as were other colorful flowers. That the creeks were full and flowing, that there seemed to be no pestilence in the planted crops.

We saw them in a cloud of dust that soon cleared and showed a whole bevy of fine-looking horses and blue-uniformed men with shiny brass buttons.

"What kind of soldiers have brass buttons so shiny?" I asked Sis Goose.

"I don't know. But we're too close to them if you can see that," she returned. "Let's go tell your pa they're here."

We galloped back toward the house and I wondered

how Pa had known they were coming. More secret connections, I supposed. Anyway, the last time Granville was home, which had been the end of May, before Granger came to Texas with his announcement of freedom for the slaves, Pa had sent a wagonload of goods back with my brother, to be shipped by boat to Bagdad, Mexico.

Mama's good silverware, tea set, and dinnerware went. So did her crystal punch bowl, her beautiful rugs, and some very special gowns and jewelry she'd been saving. A goodly portion of Pa's and the boys' books and Pa's genuine Brown Bess rifle from the Revolutionary War, along with some of his other prize guns, were loaded up.

Three good Thoroughbred horses had been tethered along the back of the wagon. Family portraits were inside it. And some special mirrors, carefully wrapped.

Mama had looked like she was about to cry, overseeing the loading of the loot, but she didn't. Granville had promised to see it all to a warehouse in Bagdad himself. The jewelry and dresses he would consign to the wife of a good friend of his in that town.

Yes, Pa had known they were coming. It was just a matter of when.

We wondered about Glen Eden and Aunt Sophie and Uncle Garland and how they would fare. But they were away in Europe, this time with my sister Amelia and her husband. "Don't worry about Glen Eden," Aunt Sophie had told Pa when he paid her a visit before she left. "Our negroes are all faithful and I've given instructions to the household women that the Yankees are to be wined and dined. A good social atmosphere does wonders. We still are all human beings," she told Pa. "And they're away from home."

Pa grumbled and told her she was daft. "They'll sit at your table and eat your meat," he told her. "Then they'll muddy your carpets, shoot your Thoroughbreds, and rip your draperies from the windows."

She would not listen, so he gave up on her.

"The only trouble," Pa concluded, "is that she's got my daughter and my fool son-in-law thinking just like her."

"Pa, the Yankees are here!" We burst in on his study without knocking.

He did not seem surprised. "All right. We'll greet them on the porch. You girls run and put on your blue cloaks."

He sure was fixated on those cloaks, like they could work some magic. But he was determined to put a good face on things.

We followed him outside. There were about twenty of them. Was that all it took? They carried their colors, the old Stars and Stripes, and a regimental flag.

On a closer look, their leader, looking up at us from his horse, was dusty and worn looking. "Name's Lieutenant Colonel Jeffrey N. Heffernan III," he said. "I and my men here aim to occupy this land for a while. Who's in charge?"

"I'm the owner," Pa said. "This here's my wife and daughters."

I saw Heffernan's gaze go over Sis Goose. His smile was a sneer, nothing less.

"My men are thirsty and hungry. You have anybody who can rustle them up some grub?"

"My servants are in the kitchen now," Pa said. "My wife'll see to it."

Heffernan dismounted and handed his reins to a slave boy. He looked at the boy, then at Old Pepper Apron in the doorway, her turbaned head, her spotless white apron. He looked into other dark faces that peered up at him.

"You free your slaves yet?" he asked Pa.

"Yes," Pa said. "These you see here chose to stay."

"You payin' 'em?"

"In accordance with government law," Pa told him. "I am."

He shot several other questions at Pa, who answered them without getting ruffled. Then he took off his gloves, slapped them against his thigh, and came up the stairs to the house. Again he looked around at the porch, the grounds, the cool interior that must have beckoned. "This'll do," he said.

"For what?" Pa asked.

Heffernan looked at Pa as if he'd taken leave of his senses. "For living," he said. "Me and my men will, henceforth, occupy this house. You and your family can move into the log house out there." He gestured across the yard.

"Looks accommodating enough. You have any problems with that?"

Pa knew when to speak and when to hold a still tongue in his head. "No, my father built that house. Likely it's stronger than this one."

"Good. Have the servants move your family out today. From here on, this place is under the command of the federal government. Go on, get moving, old man."

I started forward, toward Heffernan. To do what, I didn't know. My anger would tell me. Pa grabbed my arm just in time, but Heffernan saw my actions and gave that sneering grin of his. "What's this? A fiery little piece, I see. What's your name, little cutie?"

"Trouble," I told him. "And don't call my pa old man."

"Luli, mind yourself," Pa said. Then to Heffernan, "I ask that you respect my daughters."

Heffernan looked from me to Sis Goose. "And this little missy? She your *daughter,* too?" He emphasized the word daughter.

"She's our adopted daughter, yes. Been with us since a babe."

"A high-yellow beauty, I'd say. What can she do in the house?"

"She helps my wife all the time," Pa said.

"Good. Then she can become part of my household. My personal servant. What did you say your name is, sweetie?"

"I didn't," Sis Goose said.

"I do love the accents," Heffernan told us. "What's her name?" He looked at me.

"Rose," I said.

"Come on. I know they all have nicknames. You people have an absolute talent for giving your negroes nicknames."

"She isn't our negro," I protested. "She belongs to the family."

"Exactly. *Belongs* is the word we need. I said, what's her name?"

Sis Goose saw we were at each other's throats and interrupted. "They call me Sis Goose," she told him. "My pa named me that."

"Your pa, hey? He allow you to call him that?" he questioned.

"Her father's a steamboat captain," I told him. "And he'd kill you on sight if he knew you were making advances to his daughter. And if you hurt her in any way, I'll tell him and he'll come and kill you. Yes he will!"

I was crying by then and ashamed of myself for breaking down. The idea of this filthy Yankee living in our house tore into me.

"Men!" he called out. "Help these people move their things. You." And he pointed to Old Pepper Apron. "You're the cook. I've been on enough of these plantations to know that by now. Get in the kitchen and rustle up some grub for me and my men. Half a dozen chickens should do. And a side of beef. Potatoes and corn and whatever sweet you got on this place." He lowered his voice. "Besides these sweet little girls, that is. Sis-whatever-they-call-you, come with me. I'm in need of some drink and fruit and cheese."

He looked at Pa, who stood there helplessly. How I wished I had my gun, but it was hidden by the corn crib. Why did Pa stand for it so? How I wished Gabe and Granville were here.

"Remember," he said to us as he went through the front door. "The war is over. You're all my prisoners. The South is on its knees. See that you imitate her posture."

CHAPTER THIRTEEN

THOUGH I'D brought many a meal to Edom in the log house, I never thought about what it would mean to live there. Always it had seemed so empty, so echoing, with its bare wood floors and fireplaces of native stone.

It was made of cottonwood logs, hewn as smooth as glass, with round holes every so often to shoot a rifle out of at attacking Indians. Downstairs was a large hallway, with two large rooms on either side. The back gallery connected to the kitchen. Upstairs were two more large rooms, and soon all the place was filled up with whatever furniture Colonel Heffernan allowed us to take out of the main house.

He would allow us women only one mirror, two mule chests, and each of us one bed. Edom, who had always lived in a small back room, walked around mumbling and talking to Grandpa Holcomb as if the man were still alive.

"Good thing you're dead, Gabriel," he said to Grandpa's ghost. "Or this would kill you fer sure."

But as old as he was, he was a help in moving Pa's books into one of the downstairs rooms, and in making a study come into being.

He was free now, with all the other slaves, Edom was. But for the last ten years he hadn't lifted a finger on the place, except to sit outside and tell stories to the little negro children. Pa had been caring for him all the while.

We had nothing to cook on but the old iron skillets and pots that hung in the hearth in the kitchen. Colonel Heffernan wouldn't allow us to have Mama's brass pans or kettles. As for servants, he allowed us only Melindy and Molly and kept Old Pepper Apron and others to cook and clean for him.

Sis Goose and I wanted to cry at first, but Mama made a game of it. "Your grandpa and grandmother lived in this house under worse circumstances. At least we don't have Indians. At least we have bread and salt. Let's see if we can be as brave as they were."

But soon we had more to worry about. While Sis Goose was allowed to sleep and live with us, she was, on Heffernan's orders, to stay in the big house to be at his beck and call during the day.

She was to wait on his table. Serve him his tot of rum every afternoon on the front porch, along with cheese from the buttery and fresh plums and peaches and pomegranates from the small orchard Mama kept in front of the house.

That orchard was Mama's pride and joy. And so was Sis Goose.

And the first night of her indenture Sis Goose came home crying.

"WHAT DID that man do to you?" Mama cried.

But Sis Goose only burst into deeper crying and ran up the stairs to the room we shared together.

"Let me go," I begged Mama. "She'll tell me. Please, let me do it, Mama."

She agreed and I followed Sis Goose upstairs. She was on the edge of her bed, sobbing. I sat down next to her. "When you're ready, you tell me," I said solemnly. "I'll kill him before I let him hurt you."

She stopped sobbing for a minute, then took her hands down from her face and looked at me. "There are different ways to hurt people," she said.

I nodded yes. I told her I knew all about the ways there were to be hurt.

"Why didn't you tell me?" she said then.

"What?"

"Colonel Heffernan did. This afternoon. He told me . . . he,"—and she hiccupped—"he told me . . ."

"What? What did he tell you, Sis?"

"That I and all the slaves on this place should have been free for over two years. *Two years!* That the slaves in the states have been free all that time. He laughed at me.

He said I thought you all were so wonderful, but what kind of family keeps a member in slavery when they don't have to?"

She stood up. She glared down at me. Her nostrils flared. "All of you," she gasped. "Even Gabe." And she wailed out his name and threw herself down on the bed, sobbing even worse now.

I stood up and leaned over her. "Sis, you don't understand."

"What? What's to understand? What could there possibly be to understand? I was a slave, Luli. For two years longer than I had to be. You all could have at least told us! Over at Aunt Sophie's, she had me waiting on the table. She wanted me to clean the chamber pot! What's the matter with you people? What's wrong with you? We weren't supposed to have any secrets from each other. I trusted you!" She wailed it out and cried even more.

I was getting frightened now. Her chest was heaving, her breath coming in short spurts. "Sis," I said, and I sat down and put my arms around her.

She threw them off.

"We never treated you like a slave," I told her. "And Pa was scared that if you knew, others would know, too, and then there would be a slave uprising in Texas. War, Sis! Crops rotting in the fields. Fences down. Fruit trees ruined. We'd be back again to having no wheat for bread. Or corn. Like my Grandpa Holcomb."

Was she even listening to me?

"I trusted you," she blubbered.

"Sis, it's all over. You were treated well. Pa never would let anybody hurt you. How would it have been different if you were free?"

She stared at me. "Don't even say that, Luli. I know you aren't that stupid. I would have done things, for one."

"What?"

"Well, maybe I would have taken a trip with my pa on his steamboat. Mayhap I'd have gone to Europe with Aunt Sophie, as a free person. Who knows? But it would have been *my* choice. Mine."

"And Gabe . . . ?" I asked.

"Gabe. Oh God!" And she covered her face with her hands again. "For certain I wouldn't be carrying his child. I would have wed him properlike. For certain."

Now I felt the breath go out of me. "You're carrying his child?"

"Yes." And she gave a little laugh. "There's one for you. A secret I kept from you. How does it feel? And from him. He doesn't know. I'm only three months. And don't you dare tell anybody."

I felt something break inside me. So, it was all over then between us. I felt betrayed. But if I felt that way, how did she feel?

She gave a little laugh. "That night we spent in this very house—" and her voice broke off. "You see what I became because I thought less of myself? A white man's wench. Like my mama."

"Stop it, Sis Goose."

"My daddy was right," she told me. "In the end, that's what I am. Just a goose in a courthouse full of foxes."

There was no more to say. What could I say? Little remained between us.

"At least," she said, "the Yankee colonel up at the big house was honest with me. That's more than Gabe could be."

Then she had a thought. "You must make me a promise now, Luli."

More secrets? I shuddered. "What?"

"It can make up for your not telling me I should have been free. You can promise me that, no matter what, you won't tell anyone I'm carrying Gabe's child. *No matter what happens.* Most especially you won't tell Gabe."

A heavy promise. I sighed, wondering what I was agreeing to. But if I could make things up to her for this whole stupid family—

"Yes," I said. "I promise."

CHAPTER FOURTEEN

SIS GOOSE was full of secrets, I was beginning to learn. She carried them as if in a large bag on her back, and if you asked the right question, you could hear a pop. She wouldn't answer, but no doubt her burden got lighter.

This very night she came downstairs with some of her belongings tied in an old tablecloth.

"Where are you going?" Mama's voice cracked, because she already knew, because she likely already knew her beloved Sis Goose was moving out.

At first Sis Goose just shrugged.

"You owe Mama an answer," I said, trying to sound stern like Gabe. Sound like him? Gabe would have lifted her from her feet and carried her, wailing, upstairs.

She near whispered it. "The colonel wants me to wait on him at night, bring his drinks late while he plays cards," she said.

"We know that already," Mama said. "Just like we know he's rough and coarse. What we don't know is why you need a tablecloth full of belongings to do it."

"I know he's rough and coarse," Sis Goose returned, "but he and his men stand for freedom. I waited years to be free. And none of you told me about the slaves in the states these past two years. Not even Gabe. So Heffernan can be all the rough and coarse he wants. I'm going to wait on him, and I'm going to move to the quarters at night, where I belong."

Mama said nothing for a moment. Then she blurted out something in a strange language, a terrible language.

It sounded violent and angry. But I didn't know what it was. I never even knew my mother knew another language. Everybody in this family, it seemed, had secrets.

Then Mama went upstairs to bed.

It was my job to lock the house up every night and so I did, leaving only the back door open for when I returned. Then I took myself across the distance that separated us from our old home.

The first thing I noticed was the damage done to Mama's small front orchard. All the Bermuda grass underfoot was scuffed and marked with horses' hooves and boots.

The trees, the orange and the quince and pomegranate, the peach and plum, were stripped bare of fruit. Along the walk that led to the front steps, the pink crape myrtle and azaleas, the roses and yellow jasmine were stomped down and trampled upon.

I went up the steps and knocked on the front door of

my own house. From the front gallery I could see blazing chandeliers and hear men's laughter inside.

A private answered the door. "The butter and egg lady is here," he called out in jest.

"Who?" asked an aide, coming into the hallway.

"That bratty little kid who's been giving you all the trouble."

"Oh. Let her in."

I adjusted my eyes, going into the bright hallway. The light shone harshly on scuffed floors and ruined carpet on the stairway.

"Who is it?" A voice came from the front parlor.

"That bratty little kid who's been causing all the trouble," I told him.

"Well, don't come in here and cause any today, miss," the private said, "his honor ain't in the mood." He ushered me into the front parlor where I saw Heffernan lounging in Mama's good horsehair couch with his feet up on the Chippendale coffee table. Marks from wet glasses marred the wood. In the background the draperies on the windows hung in disarray, the secretary doors were open and coats carelessly hung on them.

The remains of supper lay on the coffee table, too, with flies buzzing around. All over the place were empty whiskey and rum glasses.

"Ho," Heffernan greeted me. "So it is. The white daughter, you mean. Come on in. What are you selling?"

"I'd like to speak to you alone," I said with all the dignity I could muster.

"Sounds serious." He pushed some newspapers from a nearby chair onto the floor. "Here, sit. You Southerners are all so damned serious."

If I had my gun, I told myself, *I'd shoot him.*

But that wasn't the way. I told myself that, too. Leastways not now, not yet. "I prefer to stand," I said.

"Sit! That's an order!" He shouted it out. Oh, he was used to giving orders all right, but if he were any good at what he did he wouldn't have to shout it.

I sat. "I have a complaint," I said.

"Against who? One of my men been making eyes at you?"

"Against you," I said bravely.

That piqued his interest. "Go on."

"You didn't have to tell Rose she could have been free two years already. Did you?"

"Who's Rose?" He looked at his aide, a Captain Cochran, sitting nearby. "You know any Rose? Why haven't I been told about her?"

Cochran gave a small smile. "Sis Goose," he said.

"Oh. The mulatto wench. And just why does that upset you?" he asked me. "If I had my way I'd shout it from the front gallery to every negro on this place. 'You could have been free over two years and those termites over at the log house didn't tell you. *Over two years. Now what are you all gonna do about it?*' Know what they'd do? Kill the lot of you in your beds at night. And it's what you rightly deserve, you hypocritical bunch of pious sewer rats."

"We didn't do anything every other planter in Texas, every slave owner in Texas, didn't do," I said. "What could we do? Let the crops rot in the fields?"

He sat forward. "Did it ever occur to those pea brains of yours to pick up a hoe and work in the fields yourselves?"

"My grandpa and pa and grandmother did that. They carved this place out of the earth itself!" I was getting heated. I wanted to cry. But I mustn't. In the name of all my ancestors, I mustn't.

He leaned forward on the couch, reached out, and took up my hand. "Look at this little paw," he said. "You've never done more than make candied violets, I'll wager."

I pulled it away. "I brush and care for my own horse. I can load a gun, clean it, and shoot it better than you can."

He roared with laughter. "We must have a shooting contest one of these days."

"I'm ready whenever you are."

"They say, sir, that her brothers taught her to shoot," Cochran put in.

He scowled. "Brothers, eh?" He becalmed himself.

"Yes. And they should be coming home soon," I told him quietly. "And when they do they'll shoot you."

More laughter. Then he went solemn on me. "Let me tell you, little girl. The war is over. Anybody shoots me now, it's murder. Three million men on our side alone died to free the likes of your Old Pepper Apron and Sis Rose."

"Sis Goose," Cochran reminded him.

"Sis Rose, Sis Goose, Sis Gander. Whatever you call her. You couldn't even give her the honesty of calling her by her own name."

"Her father named her that," I told him.

He reached onto the table for a cigar and Cochran lighted it for him. He leaned back, inhaled it, and blew out a puff of smoke. "Damn good cigars your old man has got around here. Damn good whiskey and rum and everything. You people live high on the hog and expect everybody else to do your dirty work. Well, the war's over, and we won. Time to do your own dirty work. And time I enlightened that little Sis Goose to what rotters her people are. She thought you were all so wonderful. Doesn't anymore though, does she? Moved out on you."

"She's still family," I told him.

He picked up one of Mama's good dinnerware saucers and flicked his cigar ashes into it. "I wanted her to live in this house. In her old room. She wouldn't. Said it wouldn't look right." He laughed and shook his head sadly. Then he half raised his eyes to look at me. "Family, hey? Tell me, which one of your brothers got her pregnant?"

I went white. I felt myself go weak and clutched the side of the chair. And I said nothing.

"Sir." Cochran took a step forward.

"Shut up, Cochran. Let me handle this. Well?" he put it to me again. "You got the answer to that? I've heard all about your Southern men taking midnight walks to the quarters. Whichever one it was didn't even have to go to the quarters now, did he? Had what he wanted right in the house."

"It isn't like that," I started to say.

"Oh? What's it like then? Let me tell you, little girl, in my travels in the South I thought I'd seen it all, but this—" and he waved a hand, as if there were no words to describe what he wanted to say. "This little Sis Goose girl has been treated so badly I couldn't bear the way she adored all of you and thought she was family. Would family keep her in slave labor for over two years when all her brothers and sisters back in the states were free? I had to tell her." He crushed out his cigar and stood up. "Now get the hell out of here before I really get mad. Cochran, get me some rum. I've got a bad taste in my mouth."

The interview was over. I got to my feet shakily and made my way from the room. "You wanna know what General Tecumseh Sherman of our army said?" he asked.

I stopped but did not bother turning.

"Said he wanted to bring every Southern woman to the washtubs." He shook his head. "Damn. I wish I'd said it."

CHAPTER FIFTEEN

EVERY DAY Pa asked for Sis Goose.

I had noticed that since the Yankees came he seemed more frail and kept even more to himself than usual.

He never came out of his study now and we had plenty of blue-sky days. He took the arrival of the Yankees as a personal affront aimed just at him. It became as if he himself had been beaten. Many times I caught him looking out the window of the room he now used as a study, which was in front of the log house.

He would be staring up at his old house on the slight rise a distance from us. If he saw that I caught him at this, he'd turn and shake his head and cuss softly under his breath, and tell me to sit down and keep him informed as to what was going on around the place.

"You have to be my eyes and ears," he said. "Granville and Gabe used to do this for me. Now I have only you."

We didn't tell him that Sis Goose had moved out of the house, but he knew.

"Where is our little Goose Girl?" he'd ask me. He sometimes called her that.

I had to tell him. I could never lie to Pa. "She's moved to the quarters," I said. "She's put out with us, Pa, because we never told her she was free. Colonel Heffernan told her."

"Free is what you are in your heart and soul," he said quietly. "We never treated that girl like she was anything but free. I would have given her anything. If that Sophie had allowed it, she would have been our legal daughter years ago. And as free as a soul ever could be in this world."

"Pa, don't blame yourself."

"Send her to me," he said.

"What?"

"Send her to see me. She owes me that. I want to talk to her."

His hands were shaking. They'd been doing a lot of that lately. "Yes, Pa."

"Soon," he said.

PA WAS in bed when Sis Goose came to see him. They'd moved a bed into his study, so he wouldn't have to climb stairs at night.

"Stay with me, please," Sis begged, when I turned to go.

I looked at Pa for permission. He nodded yes. So I backed away a bit and sat in a chair in the corner.

Sis knelt next to Pa's bed.

"You don't want to live with us anymore, is that it?" he asked.

Sis took his hand. She adored him, I knew that. She knew her life here all these years had come about because he succeeded in holding Aunt Sophie off from taking her back. "I'm sorry, Pa. But I was so upset when Colonel Heffernan told me I could have been free two years ago."

"And how do you like being free now?" he asked her sternly.

Tears came to her eyes.

"Is it different from before? Seems to me you're working hard these days. Look at these hands." And he took one up in his own large ones. "You never had cracked nails before. What's he got you doing? Scrubbing floors?"

"No, Pa."

"Are you happier than before?" he pushed.

She lowered her head. "No."

"Even after he goes, girl. Even after they leave and we're back in the house again, you won't find any difference than before. What do you want to do? Marry Gabe?"

She blushed. "Yes, sir."

"Did he require that you be officially free in order to marry him?"

She tried to speak and couldn't. She sobbed.

"Well, you and your Gabe will always be welcome here. It'll always be your place. Now go. I'm tired."

She sobbed some more and ran from the room.

I went over to him.

"Thought that girl had more sense," he grumbled. "Thought all the years she lived with us mattered. And what happens? Yankees come and she chooses to live in the quarters. Chooses to be one of the slaves. All the education we gave her. All the love."

"Pa, don't. You're getting yourself upset."

He laid back and I adjusted his pillow. "Feel like I'm going to die," he said. "Tell you something, Luli. You write to Gabe. Tell him to come home. Granville's likely in Mexico. Write to Gabe. Tell him I need him. Bad."

"Pa, you're making yourself sick."

"Don't talk to me like that. Impudence. You've always been impudent. You're spoiled. Those brothers of yours spoiled you."

He mumbled some things that didn't make any sense. "Get me some rum," he said.

"Pa, Mama says you shouldn't."

"I'll tell you what, little girl. I know what I should and shouldn't do. Did those Yankees leave me any rum?"

"Yes, Pa."

"Then get me some. Now."

I did so, and I stayed with him while he drank it. *I can't do this alone,* I thought. What would Gabe do? Well, I know what he wouldn't do; he wouldn't go and worry Mama. *I'll write to him,* I told myself. Tonight. And I think we ought to send a rider to get Doctor Curley. I think Pa needs him.

Doctor Curley was the one Pa sent for when a slave was really sick or dying. Scarce ever for anyone in the house. Mama knew her tried-and-true remedies.

Doctor Curley lived about an hour away on a small plantation with less than ten slaves. And we hadn't seen him since Christmas.

But he came for Pa. Like everyone in the region he had great respect for Pa, who, by that same evening, couldn't move his left arm or leg. And talked with a slur.

Pa wanted only Mercy Love, who had her own collection of remedies, and on whom he'd depended in the past. But Mama said no, she was taking charge and it would be Doctor Curley.

He told us Pa had had a stroke. "Something greatly disturbed him," he said, "and upset the natural balance of things. Must be the Yankees. That'd stick in anybody's craw."

He prescribed rest and no excitement. "I hate to make calls anymore," he said. "I haven't had any opium, turpentine, quinine, or calomel since spring of '64. Malnutrition, diarrhea, digestive disorders, and smallpox are widespread. Don't let your pa have any bad news," he said, looking at me. "When are the boys coming home?"

"Gabe will be here soon," Mama said. "Luli will write to him."

"Do you know anything special that upset him?" Doctor Curley asked.

Sis Goose, I decided; she greatly upset his natural balance. She broke his heart. But I didn't say anything.

I WROTE TO Gabe, telling him about Pa and his stroke. I used the same overland mail rider we'd used all through the war and even gave him an extra Yankee dollar. Pa had them. Again, I didn't ask from where he'd gotten them. They accomplished wonders, that's all I knew.

I didn't tell Gabe about Sis Goose and how she'd upset Pa. I did tell him, "Don't come tearing through the gates with your rifle at the ready. The Yankees are an ugly lot. Pa says we have to cooperate with them or possibly lose a lot more.

"We need you home," I told him. "Just between us, I think Pa is dying. And I can't be you, no matter how I try."

CHAPTER SIXTEEN

NO MATTER WHAT, life on the ranch had to go on.

As July approached, there were crops to bring in. Burs had to be picked off the sheep so they could be sheared for their wool. There was corn to be harvested, and it was time to plant the second round of crops: vegetables and black-eyed peas. It was also time to cut the grains: the barley, oats, and wheat. Which meant that the negroes who had stayed with us had to be managed under the new scheme of things.

Sam the faithful overseer, who'd always reported directly to Mama and taken his orders from her, managed the negros, now called *freedmen.*

Fortunately, or unfortunately, as the case may be, the men the Confederacy took from Pa's fields to dig trenches in Galveston were now coming home and must be cared for and fed. And every day the needs of the Yankees in our house had to be attended to. They liked roasted meats and would consume a whole side of beef in two days. They had first pickings at the fresh fruit from Mama's trees, the tender new vegetables. They drank plenty of rum and wine.

As we aired our log house out, swept it clean, replaced bed tickings and mosquito netting, the Yankees demanded the same services. Slavery was over, but they made us their slaves. And our needs were put in the background.

We accepted that, were even ready for it. What we were not ready for was the Fourth of July.

A WEEK BEFORE, Colonel Heffernan called us together. We stood in front of him like the negroes used to stand in front of Pa to hear his pronouncements.

"The Fourth of July is next week," Heffernan told us. "You all might remember the Fourth? It's a little holiday we like to celebrate up North. From what I understand you people had a lovers' quarrel with the North and what it stands for, several years before the war, and so decided to do away with the Fourth.

"Well, I'll miss it if we don't celebrate it here. Now I want all of you to put together a good, old-fashioned Fourth of July celebration for yourselves and for me and my men. I mean ham, fowls, and a pig with an apple in its mouth. I want chicken pies, sugar cakes, and the whole yard here lighted with pine-knot torches. I want plenty of the best preserves and jellies and cake and rum and the whole kit and caboodle. Somebody told me that the negroes here sing spirituals. That true?"

"Yeah," came a negro voice from outside the circle of whites. "We sings 'em."

"Then I want that, too. Along with 'Hail, Columbia' and 'Dixie'! Yes, 'Dixie'. Now get to work and no excuses."

Across the yard I met Sis Goose's eyes. She was standing next to Heffernan and I saw she was staring up at him, her mouth part open. I turned away, near tears.

"MAMA, DID we ever celebrate the Fourth of July?"

"Yes. Surely, you remember. We used to have all Heffernan mentioned and more."

"I don't remember."

"You mean you don't recollect your brothers pouring black powder into the bottom of an anvil and firing it off? Every year I couldn't keep you away from them doing it."

"Oh. Yes. So that's what that was for."

I was almost fifteen by now and yet it seemed as if my whole childhood had been outlined and defined by the war. Before that I couldn't recollect much, had even blocked some things out.

War had seemed the natural way of things. What human beings did. Now it was over, and I didn't know how to act, though I was ashamed to admit it.

I was helping Mama make some loaf cakes for the Fourth of July celebration. In a corner of the kitchen, Molly was churning butter. Once it was solid she would make fairy-tale figures from it, to set on the table, packed in ice.

"Mama," I said softly, so Molly couldn't hear, "I don't know how I feel about this Fourth of July. Isn't it for Yankees?"

She stopped beating the cake batter. "No. It's for you, too, Luli. Oh dear." And she wiped her hands on her apron. "I'm afraid that with all the attention we've paid to Sis Goose, we've neglected you. Just left you to grow up yourself, didn't we?"

"I had Gabe and Granville."

She came over to give me a hug. "And riding astride and camping out and firing guns at deadly creatures and bringing home deer and possum and such."

"I'm fine, Mama. It's just that I don't know what I'm supposed to feel. I hate the Yankees, the way they sit up there in our house and eat and destroy everything. Does that make them right and me wrong?"

"We can only pray all of them aren't like Heffernan," she told me. "I sense they aren't. But as far as hating them, you have every right."

"Can I still be a Southerner, and love the Confederacy, even though we lost the war?"

Tears came into Mama's eyes. "You be whatever you want to be, Luli. You are a good person. We're all good people. Because we lost the war doesn't make us otherwise."

"Then how can I celebrate the Fourth of July?"

"The same way you do everything else Heffernan says we have to do. Don't put your heart in it if you don't feel it. Only remember what your pa says. It's your country as much as Heffernan's now. You have to have some allegiance to it. And learn to be an American all over again. The laws work for you as well as for him."

"And Sis Goose?" I asked. "What do you think she's feeling?"

"God knows," Mama said. "Maybe we will know when Gabe comes home. I only pray he doesn't come home until after the Fourth."

THE FOURTH dawned clear and blue. And everything was done by the servants, exactly as every Fourth Mama ever remembered. Under the brush arbor in back of the house the long tables were set up, heavy with food.

The day before, pits for barbecuing sheep and beef, deer and wild turkey, were dug. I helped Mama make fruit pies. There was a pyramid cake made by Molly.

On the top layer, she placed a small American flag.

Heffernan had the flags, small ones and big ones, all over the place, and the red-white-and-blue bunting.

The morning of the Fourth he called me over to him at the foot of the steps to the house. Under his arm he had the bunting.

"Here." He gave it to me. "Drape it around the table. And don't let it touch the ground. I know it's not a flag, but if I see it touching the ground, I'll confine you to the house for the day."

Nothing would make me happier. I could spend the day with Pa. But Mama scowled, overhearing him. "Do as he says," she advised, "or he'll find other ways to punish us."

At high noon we had to stand at attention while Heffernan's men lined up and fired off their guns in the air in salute to the occasion. Then the dancing began, and the former slaves were allowed as much rum as they wanted.

Half in their cups, they sang for Heffernan, and we were made to stand and listen as they sang "Hail, Columbia" and "Yankee Doodle."

As it was, Heffernan punished us anyway. After Mama and I had worked all morning he would not allow us near the table until all the negro servants had come up and taken their fill. The table was near stripped bare by the time we got there.

"I'm not hungry anyway," Mama told me. "But I'll take a dish to Pa. You take one to Edom."

Mama and I took the plates of food into the cool log house to Pa and Edom. Pa ate little but snoozed away in beat with the songs in the distance. Mama sat doing some needlework. I fell asleep in the chair to the drone of Edom's voice telling how the Indians were always afraid of the negroes on those trips south that he and Grandpa made to take the cotton to the river.

We didn't see Sis Goose all night. She stayed under the brush arbor with Heffernan and his men, serving them cool drinks and listening to the songs of the negroes.

CHAPTER SEVENTEEN

THOSE SONGS, which eventually turned into mournful spirituals that most white folks seem to love so, nearly drowned out the booted footsteps on the wide-plank floors.

Two men appeared in the doorway of Pa's study, one holding a lantern so the other could see. The lantern holder was Cochran and the other man was Colonel Heffernan.

"Excuse me," Heffernan said.

In his bed, Pa's eyes flew open. "Gabe?" he asked. "Is it Gabe?"

"No, Mr. Holcomb, it's only me, Colonel Heffernan. I heard you were ailing and thought I'd come pay my respects."

Respects? I thought. Not this man. He doesn't know the meaning of the word. I didn't trust him.

He took the lantern from Cochran and set it down on a small table. "I have an offer to make to you, Mr. Holcomb. Is now not a good time?"

Pa made a gesture with his good hand that the man

should sit. Mama and I didn't offer to leave and nobody asked us to.

"It has come to my attention, Mr. Holcomb, that President Johnson is issuing pardons to Confederates who waged war against the Union. A pardon will entail taking an oath of allegiance to the Union and will entitle you to retain your lands and holdings after we leave."

Pa coughed.

"In your case, sir, a special pardon is needed since you own more than twenty thousand dollars in property. It should be personally applied for. But given the circumstances of your health I am in a position to recommend you as a good candidate for a pardon. The president hopes that with this pardon you and others like you will look upon him as your ally and protector."

"You mean people of sizeable means," Mama put in. *Good for you,* I thought. Stay one step ahead of him.

"All right, all right, Luanne," Pa slurred. "Let the man talk."

"Thank you," said Heffernan. "Well, I am in the happy position to be able to offer you that pardon, here and now, providing you take the oath."

Pa looked at Mama with some meaning in the look I could not discern. She nodded her head yes, ever so slightly. Then he closed his eyes and sighed. Candlelight in the room flickered. The negroes were singing about going home in a sweet chariot.

Heffernan shifted his weight from one foot to the other, then spoke. "Perhaps this is not a good time," he said.

"No," Pa said. "But not for the reason you think. You come back tomorrow. I have to be dressed up to take an oath."

I heard myself gasp but said nothing.

"Come by nine in the morning," Mama told him. "He's most alert then."

"He doesn't have to dress up," Heffernan said.

"Yes I do!" Pa said with as much anger as he could muster. "Don't know how you been raised, young man, but here in the South we do things right."

He propped himself up on his good right elbow to say this. Now he sank back down and waved Heffernan off.

The colonel picked up his lantern, started to say something, then stopped. It was clear that Pa bewildered him. So he said nothing and left, Cochran following behind.

I WAS WITH Mama the next day when she helped Pa tie his cravat. Edom had already shaved him and gotten him into his best and whitest ruffled shirt and black trousers. He insisted on his wool suit because the wool had all been grown on his own sheep, spun and woven by his slaves, sewn by Mama. The jacket had swallowtails, and he insisted on wearing his planter's hat on his head.

Mama handed him his gold-headed cane and he sat on the edge of his bed while Edom put on his freshly polished boots.

Heffernan and Cochran came in, and the colonel stared at Pa in amazement.

"You wait a second, young man," Pa said, his voice sounding better than last night. "I want to stand and do this thing."

Edom and Mama helped him to his feet. He reached out and took a small flag from Cochran's hand and handed it to me.

I hesitated, just a moment, and looked into his eyes.

They were pleading with me, not angry. So I took the flag and held it.

And there, in that makeshift study of Pa's, surrounded by his books, in the house his father had built in order to start the ranch, Pa took the oath of allegiance to the United States.

Heffernan said the words first. Pa followed, slowly and surely. We all held our breath.

When it was over it was clear that even stone-hearted Heffernan was moved. He cleared his throat and did not know what to say.

"You've seen the Southern training here at work, Colonel," my mama said. "But you've also seen something else."

"What is that, ma'am?"

"You've seen a man, who loves his country, embrace it unashamedly. And give good example to his children."

When she said that, Mama looked right at me. And I knew then what this was all about, really. It was about Pa's wanting to be an American again, yes, but more it was because Mama had likely told him of the trouble I'd had in knowing which was my country. And how to feel about it.

I hugged Pa and helped him sit down on the bed. He stamped his cane on the floor. "Coffee," he said, "I'll have coffee with rum in it."

"Granville, you shouldn't," Mama said.

"Lots of things I shouldn't do. Now leave me, all of you, and let Edom and me have our coffee with rum in it."

CHAPTER EIGHTEEN

A NOTE CAME to me right after that from Mercy Love down in the quarters:

"Child. Cast an eye in the direcshun of Sis Goose and that Kernal man in your old house. I hear tell from Old Pepper Apron that he has got his hands all over her. You must protect her somehow. My owl has refused to hoot for two days. He sees bad omens on this place. And I hear she carried out ashes on a Friday and this bodes no good for anyone. Come see me before you see the Kernal man and I will give you some protection. Elst wash in basil leaves to protect yourself."

AT THE SAME time came a letter from Gabe, wishing his best for Pa and telling us he'd be home directly.

During the war, it took a letter a month to travel 200 miles. Now, with the fighting ceased, it was a little better. Now the overland stage did not have to worry about being sniped at, so Pa still employed their riders to get and receive our mail.

It was one of these ragged riders who rode up to the gates that day with the letter from Gabe saying he'd be home directly. We paid him, offered him food and drink, but no, he had to get on. He had other missives to deliver.

I didn't tell Ma about Mercy Love's concerns about Sis Goose. Not with the temper I'd discovered in her. I was afraid she'd go storming into the house to ream out the colonel. I didn't care about him, but I did care that I might have another sick parent, and for that I would most certainly shoot Heffernan.

Which reminded me. Guns.

Naturally Heffernan thought he had collected all of them when he arrived, but he hadn't.

When Granville had taken all Mama and Pa's good belongings off to Mexico in the wagon, he had buried some guns out beyond the corncrib. If my recollection was correct, there was a perfectly good double-barreled shotgun buried there, and a Colt revolver. It was time to sneak out in the dark of night and retrieve them.

I WAS HAVING trouble sleeping anyway. The hot weather had brought, for me, a cold and a cough, and I had taken Mama's evil-tasting herbal medicine, boneset, to no avail. I had the fever, like Pa got off and on. But I didn't complain because then Mama would have me housebound. Still, at night I'd wake up, feverish and tossing and turning, only to find it impossible to go back to sleep again.

So I'd walk the house in slippered feet, awed by the moonlight coming in the undraped windows, listening for the sounds of the hooty owls or whip-poor-wills, every sound becoming a terror for me.

If only Gabe would come home. I'd feel safer. I wanted him as bad as I'd wanted him near when I'd had my lions under the bed.

This night there was no moon. I'd need a lantern. I dismissed the temptation to wear my boots and put on the Indian moccasins Gabe had brought home for me on his last visit. Then I picked up a lantern and went in a roundabout way to the back of the house near the quarters, where the corncrib was.

If caught, I had my story ready. I was sickly. Likely with bilious fever and was going to Mercy Love's cottage for some pills made of black pepper and opium. Best not come near me. It was catching.

Why the small shovel in my hand?

Mercy Love would most assuredly give me a red velvet bag and tell me to go to the cemetery on my way back and dig up some goofer dust just as an extra measure of protection against the disease.

Heffernan would believe anything. And he didn't interfere with any comings and goings to Mercy Love's place because he was afraid of her.

And so I made my midnight trip to the corncrib in the dark. I'd been running around the grounds here since I was two, bounding after Gabe and Granville on some adventure. I knew every hole in the ground, every tree, every bush and fence rail and path. I didn't even need the lantern, but I took it along for comfort.

Of course, Heffernan had guards posted. In front and in back of the house. But I caught two sleeping, one other in the embrace of a negro girl, and the fourth awake but drinking and likely in his cups. They posed no problem.

Luckily Granville had insisted I be with him the day he buried the guns, so I would know exactly where to go to dig them up. And luckily it had recently rained so the ground wasn't hard. I dug as soundlessly as I could. Darned Granville. Did he have to be so thorough and exact about everything?

Finally my shovel hit something and I knelt down and shoveled away the dirt with my hands. And there, wrapped in an old blanket, were the double-barreled shotgun and the Colt revolver and all the ammunition I needed.

I hauled them out, covered up the hole, and carried them, still in the earth-smelling blanket, back to the house.

In my room I examined my treasures. I got a rag and cleaned them there and then on the spot, rubbing the handles until the special carvings and the initials, GH for Pa, Granville Holcomb, were clean and clear.

Oh, how good they felt in my hands! And it came to me how I missed going out at least once a week and practicing my shooting. Now to hide them. I did so, under my mattress. I put the ammunition in an old pair of my boots in the corner and then lay down, feverish and plotting, until I went to sleep.

I DIDN'T GIVE much thought to what I was going to do, why I had gone so out of my way to fetch the guns. I knew only that it was time. That Heffernan had gone far enough putting his hands on Sis Goose, who was carrying my brother's child. The very thought of him doing it was distasteful to me. And I had to put a stop to it.

The when and how of it didn't concern me. It would all work itself out.

THE "WHEN" of it happened the next night. Again I was sleepless. The night was so nice that I wished I could open a window, so I did, just for a minute. Any longer and the room would be full of mosquitoes.

But in that minute I heard a girlish cry coming from the front gallery of our house.

Sis Goose!

This time I dressed quickly, put on my boots, took up my Colt revolver, and went out the front door.

There were lanterns lit on the front gallery. Other light shone out through the front windows onto the two of them, caught in an embrace.

"No, don't," I heard Sis Goose cry.

I crept through Mama's orchard up to the front gallery. Just to one side was a brick terrace, and there, under an orange tree, I saw Colonel Heffernan trying his darndest to get his arms around Sis Goose. She was backing away and pleading, "Don't."

"Leave her be!" I sent my voice out into the dark like a bullet, sure to hit its mark.

"Who goes there? Identify yourself." It was the guard at the front steps.

"Back off, Sergeant, I'll take care of this."

The sergeant obeyed. And Heffernan, still with one arm around Sis Goose's waist, dragged her toward the end of the terrace. He peered into the dark. "That you, Luli Holcomb? What you doing out and about this late at night? Go to bed like all good little girls."

"I said leave her be."

He saw the barrel of the Colt revolver then, pointed right at him. He laughed. "Ho, a little girl with a pistol. You Southerners really are a sight."

"She can shoot," Sis Goose said. "Don't anger her. She can shoot as good as you."

"That so?" He pushed her away, his interest piqued. He took out his revolver and aimed it at me. "What you going to do now, little girl?"

I took aim and fired. His arm. I wanted to get his upper arm. Maybe the muscle, and I must have because I heard a groan and then he bent over and clutched it. "Sergeant, get that little witch!" he yelled.

But before the sergeant could gather his wits I turned and leaped back into the blessed darkness.

Out of the corner of my eye I saw Sis Goose leaning over Heffernan, saying, "Come on into the house, we have to fix the arm."

The sergeant was there, too, helping him up and leading him in through a side door. I ran into the log house and bolted the door shut, then sank down on the floor in the front hallway. All I could hear in the silence was the beating of my own heart.

CHAPTER NINETEEN

THE NEXT morning I slept late for the first time in a long time. Sun was streaming in my room through the mosquito nets around the bed. I pushed them aside and got up to look out the window. The place was wrapped in an eerie quiet that folded around us like the mosquito netting. In the distance was the faint singing of the freedmen working in the fields, then the neighing of a horse, the barking of the hound dogs, then silence again.

No one was about. Where was Heffernan? Was he wounded? Dead? What would happen if I killed him?

I dressed quickly and went downstairs and through the back gallery to the kitchen where Mama was overseeing the making of pies. Heffernan liked pies and kept Molly busy making them. Old Pepper Apron refused to make him desserts or anything except simple meals. He was grateful for that, grateful that she wasn't trying to poison him.

Mama sliced me some ham and I reheated some muffins for breakfast. And there was coffee, real coffee. Mama was working at sorting the black-eyed peas.

She sighed. "The war is over," she said, "but around here it still goes on. I don't blame you for firing at him, Luli, but please don't fire again at the occupation officers."

"If Heffernan persists in pursuing Sis Goose, I'll kill him," I told her. "The war is over, yes, Mama, but even in peacetime Gabe or Granville would kill him for that."

"Heffernan is gone," Mama said grimly. "That subordinate of his, Captain Cochran, came 'round this morning, drank my coffee, and told me what you'd done."

"Gone? Where? Why? Not because of me."

"Cochran said he deserted."

"Well, good riddance to him."

"He took Sis Goose with him."

The words hit me like grapeshot, scattering my thoughts in a dozen directions.

She said them flat, with no feeling, and she stopped what she was doing with the black-eyed peas and faced me, wiping her hands with her apron.

"Mama," I started to say.

"She's gone, Luli. My little Goose Girl is gone."

She sat down at the table opposite me, her hands folded. "I can't even tell your father. I'm afraid he'd take a turn for the worse."

"We've got to get her back, Mama." I meant the words, though I hadn't the faintest notion how we'd do it.

She shook her head. "Don't try. Don't go after her alone. Wait until Gabe returns. He ought to be back any day now. Anyway," and she lowered her eyes, "Cochran says you're under house arrest."

"He said what?"

"We're a conquered nation, Luli. We must submit or they'll think of some horrible way to get back at us. They'll burn the house, shoot the livestock, pay off freedmen to leave. And then we'll really have nothing."

I got up. "I'm going up to the house to see Cochran," I said.

"You're not allowed out of the house. I promised Cochran I'd keep you here."

"I have a right to speak my piece. Don't worry, Mama." I started away and she put out a hand to stop me.

"Where's the gun? The one you shot Heffernan with?"

"In my pocket."

She held out her hand and I reached into the apron pocket and gave it to her. It lay there on the wooden table, like a resting animal. Mama didn't like guns, I knew, but she was accustomed to them from the boys. She had approved of my learning to shoot when I was twelve because on our place being able to shoot a snake or a wild boar was a matter of life and death.

"Watch your mouth," she said as I went out the door. "Don't sass him."

IT SEEMED so strange to use the large brass knocker on the door in order to get into my own house. A soldier opened the door and let me in. I stood in the hall, wider than it ever seemed now because most of Mama's furnishings and her good carpet were gone.

The soldier ushered me in to the front parlor where Cochran was riffling through papers on the desk they had put there. Pa's old desk. On it were empty drink glasses and food plates.

Cochran stood when I entered. "I thought I confined you to the house."

He didn't have the presence that Heffernan had had, the presence of command. And his voice was too high-pitched. Wrong for the job. I'd be willing to wager that in real life he'd been a schoolteacher or a store clerk, who'd never had reason to carry a gun.

"They say you are a fair man," I lied, "and will hear me out."

He nodded, flattered. Heffernan would never allow himself to be flattered. Cochran gestured that I should take a seat, then sat down himself.

"What you did was a criminal act," he said with some firmness, like a teacher scolding a student because his arithmetic answers were wrong. "I should bring charges against you. But now I have a fugitive commanding officer to deal with, and all I want for the moment is for you to be under house arrest. Later on in the day I'm going to post guards around the cabin."

I nodded. "He was making advances toward Sis Goose. I couldn't abide that. My brother left Sis Goose in my care until he gets back. And he'll be back soon. And he pointed a gun at me. It was self-defense. My brother wouldn't have aimed for the arm. He'd have killed him."

"Then it would be murder," he said.

"A matter of honor in these parts."

He fooled with some paper on the desk, lowering his gaze. "You're very adult. Who taught you to shoot?"

"My brother Gabe. Where did Heffernan go with Sis Goose?"

"Don't you think I wish I knew? I'd send men after him. But I can't spare men when I don't know for certain where he's headed."

"Does he know anybody in Mexico?"

"No. New Orleans, yes. But still I can't be sure enough to justify sending my soldiers out."

I nodded. Turned out he *was* a fair man.

"I'm going to have to confiscate your gun," he said. "I thought we had them all. I suppose you had the gun hidden somewhere."

I nodded yes.

"What else have you got hidden?"

"Nothing." That was the truth. Everything was in Mexico.

"You Southerners are a mystery to me," he said. "Up home a young girl like you would still be learning to embroider. And these slaves, I mean freedmen, could walk off and more than half have stayed. Just about all your household help stayed. That cook in the kitchen is a specimen that deserves study." He shook his head wonderingly.

"Go back to the house now. And stay there. I've got to have complete command around this place or there will be chaos. Would you cooperate with me, please?"

I stood up. "What do you do when you're not in the army?"

"I teach school in Philadelphia."

I nodded. "You're going to have to negotiate with my brother Gabe when he comes home."

"I've dealt with worse."

I felt satisfied. There was a quiet, underlying determination in him after all. I was glad I'd come. I could explain him to Gabe.

At the door his voice stopped me. "How is your father?"

I turned. "Middling well."

"Give him my regards and tell him not to worry. I'll keep order around here."

"We don't want him knowing that Sis Goose is gone. He'd take a turn for the worse."

He nodded. "Right. Now I'm going to send a man to the house later for any other guns you have. Please don't make trouble."

I promised I wouldn't and I left. What I'd accomplished, I didn't know. But Pa always said that you should know and respect your enemy.

That afternoon a soldier came for the guns. I gave them to him, the Colt and the shotgun, and I didn't make any trouble.

The next day Gabe came home.

CHAPTER TWENTY

IT WAS LATE in the afternoon when he came. I was in the parlor with Mama, who was going over the books.

"Thanks to the freedmen who stayed and worked the fields we're going to be solvent this year. Just barely," Mama said.

"What about the money Pa has in England?" I asked.

"When Gabe comes home your father will give him authority to get it. There's no telling when Granville will come. I'd be willing to wager he's going to stay in Mexico a while."

"Mama, is Pa going to die?"

I was working on a sheet of paper, adding up the bales of cotton that would be shipped to Mexico this year. She looked up at me.

"He isn't that well, Luli. So yes, he may soon die."

"What will happen to us then?"

"The boys will be home. And I'll be glad to relinquish the running of this place to them."

"And me? What will happen to me?"

"I suppose the boys will want me to send you to school in Virginia now that the war is over. Don't you want that?"

I shook my head vigorously no. "After all we've been through here I couldn't abide a silly girls' school, Mama. Especially in Virginia. They'd make me ride sidesaddle there. And never shoot a gun."

"We've all spoiled you." She smiled. "We'll see."

"Now that the war's over there will be plenty of people coming south. Can't I just have a better tutor here?"

"Go and make us some tea. I'll discuss it with the boys."

I got up. "Granville will say no. Gabe will say yes. What then, Mama?"

"We'll see who your father names to run things."

I thought of Granville washing my mouth out with soap.

"Lord, I hope it's Gabe." I went out back through the gallery and into the kitchen. There was usually a kettle of water over the fire in the hearth. I was just getting a tray and two cups and setting them down on the table when I saw a shadow across the floor and heard a voice.

"Better make that three cups. And I'll have coffee."

I looked up.

He stood there in the open doorway, backlit by the sun, his boots dusty and worn, his uniform the worse for wear. He held his hat under his arm, military fashion.

"Gabe!"

I hugged him and he enveloped me in his arms, hard. "You just get here?"

He gave a short laugh. "Yeah. If not for your letter, I'd have gone up to the big house and walked right in. They wreck the place much?"

"Some. Oh, Gabe, I'm so glad you're here. Come on in. I'll make some coffee."

"Where's Ma?"

"In the parlor, working on the books."

"Where's Sis Goose? I thought she'd be right here to greet me."

Oh dear God, I remembered then that he didn't know. I must have looked stricken because he went grim. "What's wrong, Luli?" he asked in a tone that brooked no lies.

"She's gone," I blurted out. "She was taken by Heffernan, the colonel."

"Gone? What in hell do you mean gone?"

So I told him. Everything. He listened gravely, then said in disbelief, "You shot Heffernan?"

"Yes. He was making advances toward Sis Goose."

"So he's wounded then. How far can he go? Come on, get that coffee. Here, I'll help. I want to see Ma and plan strategy."

He hid his grief well. I suppose after fighting Indians, after long hours spent riding through the mesquite-covered ground and under a blazing sun, keeping watch for Kickapoos who were always on the warpath, that he was good at hiding his feelings.

Or, at least, directing them into plans. He didn't waste time mourning.

Mama was absolutely daft, seeing him, of course. Tears came down her face and she kept saying, "My boy, my boy," and patting his face and his shoulder.

We had our repast. I'd brought some sliced ham and biscuits, fruit and cheese in the parlor for Gabe, who was starved as usual. Then, when we spoke of the war, the Yankees, and Pa, Mama looked at me.

"Luli, go upstairs and see your father. Tell him Gabe is home. I don't want him to be shocked. We'll be up directly."

They wanted to talk alone. I understood that. So I did as I was told.

I SAT WITH Gabe's captain's jacket on my lap and maneuvered the pair of scissors carefully.

Gabe had given me the job of cutting off the insignias of rank from the shoulders. None of his civilian clothes fit him anymore. All the shirts and jackets were too tight. He'd grown in the shoulders and chest. When he'd gone up to the house to pay his respects to Cochran he was ordered to cut off the captain's insignias if he wanted to continue wearing the uniform.

I remembered how proud Mama had been when she'd sewed them on. And as I cut carefully through her stitches,

I remembered the conversation between Gabe and Captain Cochran.

"I want you with me," Gabe had said to me. "I'll see if I can get rid of this house arrest thing. Get you put in my recognizance."

"What does that mean?"

"It means that I'm responsible for you. That it's a matter of my honor that you don't run off. And that I bring you back when we go looking for Sis Goose."

I couldn't believe my good luck. "You're taking me with you?"

"I need you with me. For Sis's sake. But I have to get Cochran's permission. So come along and don't mouth him. Be quiet and respectful. If he's a decent sort, as you say, I can negotiate with him for some shotguns to take with us."

I WAS SURPRISED to see Gabe salute as we went into the parlor where Cochran had set up his office. Cochran stood and returned the salute and told him to sit.

These people, I thought in wonder. Put a uniform on them and they all act the same, like they've read some special bible written just for them.

"I'm here to negotiate a few things," Gabe said.

Cochran nodded.

"First, with your permission, I'd like to ride out and find Colonel Heffernan. I can't have him running off with my intended."

"I suppose we could manage that," Cochran said.

"You can send as many or as few men as you want with me. I'll be subject to their command."

Cochran shook his head. "I have no men to spare. I'd have sent them already if I did." He took a sheet of paper and began scribbling, then signed it and shoved it across the desk at Gabe. "In case anybody stops you," he said.

Gabe folded the paper carefully and just as carefully said, "There's one more thing."

"There always is," Cochran said quietly.

"I'd like to take my sister with me. I'd be totally responsible for her. Put her in my recognizance. I promise, as a matter of honor, to bring her back."

This time it wasn't so easy. Cochran leaned back in his chair again. He ran his hand along his very narrow beard, and I could see he'd made serious decisions before. "Honor, hey?"

"Yes, sir."

"Is there a reason for this besides the fact that I'd probably put her in stocks before you returned?"

Gabe started to smile, then caught himself. "Yes. She and Sis Goose grew up together. They have some women's understanding there between them. You know what I'm talking about, Captain?"

Cochran rolled his eyes. "Oh yes, I know."

"So you'll let me take her then?"

Cochran reached down on the floor and fetched a bottle of rum and two glasses. The other request had been easy. This was too much for him. He poured two glasses and shoved one across the desk and Gabe drank his down in one gulp.

Cochran leaned back in his chair, closed his eyes, put his hands across his midriff and stayed that way for about two minutes. I glanced at Gabe, concerned. He waved me off. Then he spoke.

"How's the ranch holding up, sir?" he questioned casually.

Cochran didn't open his eyes. "Right well. Right well. Great person, that Sam. Look, out of respect for your mother and father, I can promise you nothing will be destroyed." Now he opened his eyes. "Maybe when you come back, you can take over around here. Your mother is getting tired. Under my jurisdiction, of course."

"Fine," Gabe agreed. "I was hoping for that."

"The girl is a handful. I don't know what to do with her," Cochran said.

It hit us both like grapeshot. But Gabe never missed a beat.

"I can handle her," he returned quietly. "My brother and I practically raised her, what with my father being sick and my mother running the ranch."

Cochran was somewhat mollified. Then, "I'm sorry, but I can't allow you to wear that uniform."

Silence from all of us. Cochran looked embarrassed for a minute, Gabe indignant, but he kept his demeanor. "Nothing else fits me," he said.

"Well then, wear it, but you have to remove the captain's insignia on the shoulders."

Gabe promised he would. And then he asked for the rifles.

"Before I allow you to go on this expedition, or give you the required rifles, you'll have to take the oath of allegiance to the United States."

I heard Gabe clear his throat, then say he would. I wasn't surprised. No doubt when he'd visited Pa he'd been told about how Pa had taken the oath. Pa would, I know, have left it up to Gabe, but I also knew that given Pa's example, Gabe would do it.

I stood beside Gabe. Quietly and without faltering, he took it. Then the two of them shook hands.

Cochran looked at me. "I'm remanding you to your brother's recognizance," he said. "He's promised you'll behave. Any more monkeyshines like you pulled before and there will be no leniency. I'll prosecute you to the full extent of my authority. Do you understand?"

"Yes, sir." I called him "sir" because Gabe had. And because I sensed he liked it. And because I was Southern.

That afternoon we made all the arrangements for our trip, right down to the piece of dried buffalo meat we each carried tied to our saddles.

CHAPTER TWENTY-ONE

Mercy Love said that the quarter moon last night was dripping blood. And this was a bad omen.

Her owl still hadn't hooted. He just stared at you with that owl's accusing stare, his eyes finding you guilty for things you hadn't even done yet.

I paid Mercy Love a visit as part of getting ready for my trip. She gave me an anklet made of silver coins to wear as protection against picking up evil. She made it herself, and to make it more powerful, had soaked the coins for thirty minutes in the entrails of a living frog.

She offered up in a smoking fire an ounce of gunpowder mixed with whiskey to calm Gabe's heart and give him power. Then she brewed me some tea made of dogwood roots, and I left feeling a lot better about things. Gabe didn't visit her. He was of the usual male persuasion, which was to doubt her seriously. Yet he respected the things she did for him and always sent his thanks.

The next visit I made was to Pa.

He was lying back on his pillows, looking wan. Mama had told him about Colonel Heffernan taking Sis Goose, and we were afraid it was the final blow for him. He didn't look as if he would last the day. But with Gabe by my side, I soothed him.

"Bring her back," he told us.

Gabe promised him he would. And every time Gabe discussed Sis Goose, I felt ashamed and embarrassed. For he didn't know about the baby. And I couldn't tell him.

I kissed Pa and he held me as close as he could. His body seemed frail. Tears were coming down my face as I turned back to Gabe, who gestured I should leave the room. He had business with Pa before we left.

Before we left meant there might not be a pa when we came back. For Gabe had some legal-looking papers in his hand that Pa had given him.

"Power of attorney," he called it later. It meant he was authorized, in all things legal, to act in Pa's name. To recall the money from England, which he did by letter that same day. He was in charge of the ranch. Gabe's word, not Cochran's, was final and legal. And he was in charge of me.

Granville had all his interests in Mexico, though he would occasionally come home.

Gabe and Pa were in Pa's bedroom quite a while. When he came out, Gabe looked white in the face, older, solemn. And then he went to consult with Mama in the parlor.

I packed my things. I went into the kitchen of the big house, with Cochran's permission, to secure some food for us from Old Pepper Apron.

I had always been, like everyone else on the place, a little afraid of Old Pepper Apron. When I was a child of about six, and Sis Goose was nine, we'd bother her for sweets in the kitchen.

All we had to do was walk in for her to scold us. "What you want in my kitchen, you two little spawns of the devil? After my cookies again?"

She had jars of cookies: sugar, spice, peppermint, even chocolate. And she always had dishes of peppermint and taffy candy. No fancy candied violets for her. She stuck to the real thing.

"Well, hurry up, I haven't got all day. I'm making this roast for your pa." She'd watch over us closely and allow us to select a few choice cookies or candies, then usher us out. I didn't want to leave. Her pots on the hearth and on the old woodstove were bubbling with good-smelling things to eat. I wanted to stay and learn to make things like she did. So did Sis Goose.

She was kinder to Sis Goose than to me. Which was why she was so kind to me this day, having heard we were going to fetch her home.

"You bring that girl home to me and I'll never scold her again. Allow her to have all the sugar cookies she wants," she said.

And with all the other food she gave us there was a special package of sugar cookies just for Sis Goose.

The other food was traveling food. Gabe had given

me a list. Since we were taking not only food but a tarpaulin, in case of hail, and pine knots for light at night, and blankets, a fry pan and coffee pot, and bags of corn in case we had to trade with Indians, we were taking along a pack mule.

The food Old Pepper Apron gave me complied with Gabe's list. She liked and respected Gabe.

Berries, salt pork, sweet potatoes, coffee, sugar, biscuits, bread, bacon, onions, dried beef jerky, and even some eggs, "'Cause I know how much he likes his eggs," Old Pepper Apron said. She wrapped them in cotton. She even sent along some hard candy. Gabe had his usual flint and steel to start fires.

"Are we going to be gone that long?" I asked Gabe.

He chose not to answer.

I HAD OTHER questions for him as we started out, south by southwest, according to Gabe's charts.

"Did Pa put you in charge of everything?"

"Yes."

"Do you think Granville will be put out?"

"Hardly. Likely he'll be relieved."

"Does that mean you're not going to fight Indians anymore?"

"Don't ask so many questions."

We rode in silence. I gave him that, since he seemed to have a lot on his mind. I noticed he'd paid a visit to

Captain Cochran before he left, likely to tell him he, not Ma, would be dealing with him on matters of the ranch from here on in.

Then he asked me a question. "Are you afraid?"

"Am I supposed to be?"

"Don't sass me, Luli."

He was in charge, all right.

CHAPTER TWENTY-TWO

WE FORDED several springs that first afternoon and saw many stray cows roaming the prairie that seemed to go on forever. Gabe said we were on what was called a thicket prairie, named for its clumps of dwarf dogwood and plums, all tangled together, and its wild grape full of snakes.

"Ma would like those plums for jelly," I told him.

"Well, we're not stopping and saying please to those snakes," he shot back. "Look up ahead at the flowers."

I gasped. The ground up ahead was filled with blue salvia and it went on and on until the coreopsis took over, then the verbenas, which gave way to the larkspur, the standing cypress, and then as far as I could see the French pinks.

"Oh, I wish Ma could see!" I breathed.

Next came the post oak and cottonwood trees, and then the water hole where we stopped so our horses could drink, after which Gabe found the trail he was looking for that would lead us to Cummin's Station, a trading post where he said we could stop tomorrow to ask questions.

We were a goodly amount of miles from civilization when we halted that first night as the sun set. I was in charge of roasting the sweet potatoes. Gabe said we should eat the smoked chicken. And we had berries and fresh coffee for dessert.

Sunset always makes me sad and seizes me with loneliness. And though I was in the company of Gabe, probably my most favorite and dependable person in the world, I felt homesick and missed Ma and Pa. I wanted to be in our kitchen at home where the good smells were. I was silent, eating. Gabe glanced across the fire at me.

"You ailing?"

"No." Was he asking because he cared? Or because it was his job now? Why did I have to torment myself? Couldn't I take things at face value?

"Sorry you came?"

"I miss Ma and Pa."

"Course you do. But think of it this way. You're doing this for them. Bringing back Sis Goose."

I nodded and smiled. "Thank you," I said. "I forgot that."

He eyed me. "You're a good kid. The way you always think of Ma, like back there with the plums and the flowers. I was a bit scared at first that you were going to give me a run for my money, but now I'm glad Pa put me in charge."

This took me by surprise and embarrassed me. "Can I have some coffee?"

"Ma let you have coffee this late at night?"

"Yes."

He nodded yes and poured it for me, and somehow when I tasted it I felt closer to Ma and her kitchen, and the enormous open sky over me didn't seem so overwhelming.

This then was our first night out and where I began my story.

As I SAT ruminating about matters that had brought us here and listening to the even breathing of Gabe coming across the fire, I heard a twig snap. A small animal scurried outside the rim of firelight and the branches of a nearby oak tree groaned as if under the weight of some slinky animal that got slinkier and bigger as the moments went on.

I heard the troubled *who-whooo* of a great horned owl. Then the cackling laugh of a little screech owl. It all reminded me of Sasquach, Mercy Love's owl, and with my boots off I was able to finger the ankle bracelet she had made me out of coins.

"What the devil is that thing?" Gabe asked.

"Mercy Love made it for me. To ward off evil. You'll never guess what she soaked the coins in."

"I don't think I want to."

"Well, she burned a small fire of gunpowder and whiskey for you to be calm and to have power."

He yawned. "See anything tonight?"

"No, but there's some kind of animal up there in that big tree. I hear the branches groaning from its weight."

"You calculate what kind it is?"

"A wild bobcat."

"Most likely a Mexican cougar."

"We're not in Mexico."

"You tell him that."

"Oh, Gabe, what'll we do?"

He laughed. "There's nothing up there, Luli, but a good piece of your imagination."

"Gabe, I'm scared."

He grinned. "Good. I wouldn't want anybody with me who didn't know enough to be scared. Keeps you alert."

"Are you scared?"

"I'm always scared, Luli. Out on the trail, searching for Kickapoos, but mostly inside, having polite conversation with polite folks."

I stared at him. "Even in our house?"

"Most especially in our house, yes."

"But why? Pa's made you boss now. Everybody has to listen to you."

"For just that reason, I'm scared. Think about it. I'm responsible for the ranch, though Cochran runs it. Pa is dying. Ma looks as if she is. We've got to turn a profit every year or go under. I've got this business with Heffernan, and then there's you."

"Me?"

"Yeah. Think I'm going to build those stocks Cochran was talking about and keep them for when you have bad days."

He smiled. I didn't. I felt tears in my eyes and stared hard, straight ahead.

"Hey, c'mon," he said. "What's wrong, eh? You're different from before I left for the war."

"I was just trying to find out what you're afraid of," I snapped.

"The things that scare me can't be seen or heard, Luli," he said sadly. "And I'm not ashamed to admit it. But now, why don't you go to sleep. It'll be dawn in about six or seven hours."

I had been waiting for him to mention Sis Goose in the conversation. He never did.

I slept. He didn't tell me until the next morning that what had been up in the tree were buzzards. Waiting.

"For what?" I asked.

"What do they wait for?"

I didn't say it but I knew. For people to die.

THE NEXT day the trail he had found ended. And after an early breakfast and an early start we traveled over ground covered with mesquite, prickly pear, and then some buffalo grass. The prairie was endless, and when I looked at the flat line between earth and sky it seemed to go on forever. And then, there in the distance, loomed a high mountain region studded with peaks of lime shell and chalky rocks. The scenery was breathtaking, and Gabe smiled seeing me mesmerized by it.

"See that tall tree over there? The swallow-tailed

hawks build their nests on the tallest branch that will bear the weight. The eggs are the best you'll ever eat. We'll stop a short distance away and, while you keep watch, I'll climb up and try to get some eggs."

I watched, rifle at the ready, while he climbed the tree and came down carefully, cradling two large eggs. "We'll eat them for supper with some salt pork," he promised.

I put them away in the cotton with the few we had left over from home.

We didn't halt for lunch but ate some dried buffalo meat we had tied to our saddles. We made a brief stop so the horses and mule could water.

And for us, we paused only once so we could modestly relieve ourselves within a distance of each other. Then we went on.

We had been riding quite a while and needed a rest, so when we came across a large plum patch and saw the delicious fruit on the bushes, Gabe suggested we stop and refresh ourselves with a treat.

I was just biting into the soft and sweet, yet tart, fruit when Gabe pushed his foot around on the ground. "Someone's been here before us," he said.

There were fresh plum skins on the ground.

Just then we both looked up to see a magnificent stallion approaching with an Indian and little boy riding him.

"Comanche," Gabe whispered. "Down."

I hit the ground hard, after reaching for my shotgun. Gabe had told me that Comanches were always on the warpath, and I found myself shivering with fear.

Gabe crouched over me. "Don't shoot," he whispered. "There're only two of 'em. But why should a man dressed like a chief be riding with a little boy like that? Something's not right."

He stood up. They had seen us. And it was then that I discovered one more of my brother Gabe's talents.

He spoke Comanche. As well as the Kickapoo and Delaware languages.

The man was dressed like a chief, for what little I knew, complete with feathers and beads. The little boy was about ten and wore a buckskin shirt and leggings trimmed with handsome beads.

Gabe came out of the brush and talked to him for a while. Then the little boy came forward to gather more plums.

"Chief is blind," Gabe told me. "The boy is his guide."

"What did you ask him?"

"If they'd come across a Yankee officer and a young girl riding around these parts. He pointed south past Pond Creek. There's a steam mill at Pond Creek. We'll ask there after we ask at Cummin's Station."

"So he's friendly, then?"

"Yes, we're in luck. Here, let's clear out and let 'em have more plums."

We left them eating to their heart's content. And Gabe left a small sack of corn, difficult to get in these parts, and you'd think we'd given them a sack of gold.

That day we traveled near twenty miles. We saw plenty of wild game, dusty black buffalo, deer, antelope, wild mustangs, even some real Mexican lions.

Gabe knew how to bypass them all. We passed a large spring that Gabe said gushed out twenty barrels of water a minute.

He'd been this way before. On a trip to Mexico with Granville when he was young. Before the war. "Thank heaven the country doesn't change," he said. "I remember it like it was yesterday."

We stopped at the end of the day at a place called Boone's Creek. Gabe said the creek held rare unio shells. "They're mussel shells that give a large share of pearls," Gabe told me. "When we were here, Granville dove in and got himself some pearls and gave them to a girl he knew in Mexico. I'm going in."

And before I knew it, he'd stripped to his smallclothes and was in the cold water, looking for the shells with the pearls in them.

"You might as well wash," he said. "It isn't too cold."

I took off my skirt and blouse and, in my chemise and pantalets, I found myself some privacy in a cove and had a good wash, with some lavender soap Mama had sent along.

Gabe did find one shell that yielded a pearl.

"It's for Sis Goose," he said.

It was the first time since he talked with the Indian that he'd really spoken of her on this trip.

THERE WAS a lot of petrified wood around and Gabe collected some and started a fire. I sat next to it, drying my hair with a piece of flannel. Gabe cooked the swallow-tailed hawk eggs and salt pork, which was the most delicious supper, along with his strong coffee, that I ever had.

The sunset was beautiful. The coffee perked. And I felt strangely safe and brave out here on the prairie with Gabe, though I still missed home. Then he started to talk.

"In New Orleans, on Christmas, roses are in bloom and trees are in full green leaf," he said.

But what was he saying? I looked at him questioningly.

"You'd like New Orleans," he said.

I just stared at him across the fire.

"Luli, I'm thinking of putting you in school in New Orleans after all this is over and the dust settles. The ranch won't be the same until the Yankees leave. And it looks as if they've dug in for a while. You have to further your schooling."

I was speechless. New Orleans?

He cleared his throat. "Pa told me he wanted you to have more education. And I know you don't like the idea of Virginia. Unless you want to go to Miss Trask's School for Young Ladies in Cole's Settlement near Brazos."

I shook my head no, vigorously. "That's a silly-boots school like Virginia. I don't want to go away anywhere, Gabe. I can learn everything from a good tutor at home."

"Not everything you need to know," he said firmly.

"For what?"

"For life."

"I can shoot a gun and skin a deer and cook it. I can ride better than any woman."

"Someday you'll marry. Well, we hope. And there are things you need to know to be a wife to a man of good standing."

"Mama can teach me."

"Don't argue with me, Luli. I've made up my mind. It's either New Orleans or Miss Trask's. I've been to New Orleans. There's a fine school there for young ladies of eminence. And it's closer to home than Virginia. Also, I don't know how we're going to be regarded in the states now that the war is over."

"I don't want to turn out like Amelia."

"Nor do we want you to. Now it's settled. You've time yet. I just wanted to prepare you."

Everything inside me was wringing out, like the servants wrung out the clothes on washday. I could see myself, flat and lifeless, already hung on the drying line.

"You do it for Pa," he said, "if not for me."

Pa. He was wily enough to use that on me. He knew I couldn't say no to Pa, especially now that he was dying.

Then, as if the whole matter were settled, he gave the conversation a new turn.

"Tell me, did you ever tell Sis Goose over these last two years that she was free?"

The question hit me between the eyes.

"You never mentioned Sis Goose once, all the way down here, until Boone's Creek. And now you do it to take my mind off that stupid school in New Orleans."

I saw anger cloud the blueness of his eyes. "You're going to that school, Luli. Don't fight me on it. I don't lose well. Matter of fact, I seldom lose at all. Now answer my question, please. Did you ever tell Sis Goose that she was free?"

"No. I lied to her like everybody else did."

He nodded slightly. "Is she upset that I didn't tell her?"

I didn't spare him. "Yes."

"Do you think that's why she left with Heffernan?"

Another shot between the eyes. "He kidnapped her. She didn't leave."

"Are we sure of that? What did she say to you?"

"All she said was that if the Yankees were for freedom she wanted to be with them up at the house."

"Exactly," he mused. Then, "Well, it's something we'll have to find out, isn't it?"

I didn't answer. He seemed bitter. Would Sis Goose have gone with Heffernan of her own will? But she loved Gabe, didn't she? Can love change its color like that, one minute standing for one thing, the next for something else?

I had the first watch. Gabe rolled over and went to sleep, and I sat back, leaning on my saddle, and tried to find some answers in the stars. In the distance wolves howled out their sad song.

And then, for no good reason in the world, I started to cry.

It was like losing my supper because all the sadness of the last few weeks churned in my innards and I couldn't keep it from erupting. It just came out, the business with the Yankees in our house, Pa dying, my having to dig up the guns and shooting Heffernan, and finally, now, the crowning touch that invaded my being tonight.

Having to go to school in New Orleans. Leaving home and Mama and Sis Goose. Would I even be here for her and Gabe's wedding?

The quiet flow of tears quickly turned into an overflow, like some of the springs we'd forded, swollen because of the rain.

Because then came the sobs. I couldn't stop them once they started. At first I tried to stop them, fearful they'd wake Gabe and he'd think I was a sissy boots. And then soon I didn't care.

"What's wrong?" asked a worried Gabe, suddenly standing over me. "You ailing?"

"No-ooo."

"You don't have that business that girls get . . . you know."

"What business?" But he was rubbing his face, not looking at me. Oh, I would make him pay for New Orleans. "What business?" I asked again.

"You know. That business girls have to deal with every month."

"Oh, no."

"Well, stop that fool crying, then. Come on, Luli, stop it and tell me." He pulled out a large red handkerchief, the kind men use on the prairie, and knelt down beside me and wiped my face. "I spoke too soon. You *are* going to give me a run for my money, aren't you?" he said quietly.

I couldn't help smiling. Then I hiccupped and couldn't stop.

"Lord. You used to do that when you were a baby. Drove Ma crazy. Here." He picked up his flask, uncovered it, and offered me a sip. I shook my head no.

"You think I'm going to stay up all night nursing your hiccups, you're daft, girl. Take some. That's an order."

"You think"—I hiccupped—"you're still in the army."

"Right. I'm the captain and you're the private. Drink."

I drank. I almost spit it out, but he wouldn't let me. He held my head back and put his hand over my mouth. "Swallow."

I did. For a good two minutes, he held my head like that. Then he let me go and the hiccups were gone. I breathed. “That’s worse than when Granville washed my mouth out with soap,” I said.

“Don’t use Granville’s name in vain. He’s a little rough around the edges, but if he were in charge you wouldn’t be so spoiled.”

“I’m not spoiled.”

“That’s a matter of conjecture. At least you’re not crying anymore, are you? Now tell me why you *were* crying.”

So I told him, between sighs and diminishing sobs.

“Hey,” he said, “I know it’s been rough going. And you’ve held up all along. And don’t think I don’t appreciate how you took care of Ma and Pa while I was away. And how you took care of Sis Goose. Come on now, you’re not going to start with the tears again, are you? Hey, know what I think you need?” He pulled my hair.

“Stop it.”

“I think you need a funny and interesting story. Did you know that coyotes like to eat hats and shoes?”

“No.”

“You’d better watch out. You’re liable to lose yours. Why don’t you put them under your saddle when you go to sleep later? I do.”

I hadn’t noticed him doing it, and I wondered if this was just another trick to get me to stop crying. But he looked so earnest, so serious about it that I said, all right, I’d do it. And I’d stop crying, too. So he returned to his bedroll and went back to sleep.

When my watch was over, I took off my boots and put them, with my hat, under my saddle so the coyotes wouldn't get them. I felt silly doing it, but I had seen Gabe do it with his.

Later on that night, I felt someone moving around me and squinted into the tricky darkness. There was Gabe, taking my hat and shoes out from under my saddle. I watched as he walked off and hid them in some high grass a little ways from our camp.

He's really going out of his way to amuse me, I decided. And I was touched by it, after all the trouble he had right now.

IN THE MORNING he made a great show out of telling me his hat and shoes were gone. Taken. And then he came and lifted my saddle from the ground. Mine were gone, too.

"How did the coyotes lift my saddle and get them?" I asked. I wasn't about to let him off easy.

"Don't know. It's one of the mysteries of this wild country. There are a lot of mysteries out here. I'm going to look around and see if they dropped them anywhere."

I was intrigued, wanting to see what he would do next, how far he would go with the joke. And my troubles were temporarily forgotten.

I followed him about while we looked around the camp. Then he went into the high grass where I knew he'd put them last night.

They were gone, both our sets of boots. The hats were there but torn to pieces.

The grass was trampled down around the torn-up hats. The coyotes had been and gone.

Gabe scratched his head. Wordless he was, for the first time since I'd known him.

I laughed and he scowled at me. "What's so funny?"

"The story. I didn't believe you. Until now. The coyotes took them, our boots."

But I couldn't stop laughing. He looked so funny standing there in the tall grass in only his socks. I nearly collapsed, laughing.

I whirled around, still laughing. I couldn't stop.

"What in purple hell is wrong with you?" he demanded.

"Your story. It came true. You were just telling it as a story. I saw you last night, taking my hat and boots from under my saddle and hiding them in the tall grass to make me believe the coyotes took them and now the coyotes *really* did *take them*! Oh God! It's all too much. I can't help it."

He started toward me and I ran. I ran fast, but he was pursuing me. I hurt my feet on some stones on the ground, but I kept going because he was gaining on me. And then I fell and he was on me, pulling me up and turning me around and shaking me.

"I made myself a vow, when I took on this guardian thing with you," he said, "that I'd never hit you. No matter what you did. I promised Pa I'd be gentle with you."

There were tears in his eyes. I had pushed him to the edge.

I hugged him impulsively around the waist to comfort him. Overhead a giant hawk circled. "Did the coyotes really come?" I asked.

"Yes."

"You have powers, Gabe."

"Well," he put me at arm's length, "I'm glad to see you're your own sassy self again."

The hawk was circling close over us now, closing in, like the truth of the matter was closing in on Gabe. "You going to tell anybody about this?" he asked.

The temptation was too much. I could tell people and embarrass him, or I could keep a still tongue in my head and never mention it again. The best part of it was that he knew I could tell so I had it to hold over him. And hold it over him I would, as punishment for his deciding to send me away to school. Telling wasn't the point.

It was the threat that mattered. And Gabe knew it. And I would always have it. Like Pa had had his money in that English bank.

I looked up at him. Into those blue eyes, that were as endless in scope as the prairie itself.

"It can be our secret if you behave yourself," I told him sassily.

"So you've got something on me."

"Yes."

"Vows can be broken, you know."

We both laughed on our way back to camp, then discussed the bigger problem. What to do with no boots. We decided to wear our Indian moccasins. "We ought to reach Cummin's Station today," he said. "It's a good trading post. They'll have boots. Come on, let's pack up."

CHAPTER TWENTY-THREE

WE WERE five or six miles from Cummin's Station. And the way we had to travel was free of obstacles, because Cummin's Station was ten miles above San Felipe, Gabe said, and so we'd be passing a scattering of plantations, tilled land, and lovely green pasturelands.

We did the six miles the next morning under skies as blue as Mama's porcelain and as we came upon Cummin's Station in the distance, Gabe slowed his horse's pace and I followed. The trading post was bigger than I thought it would be, and outside were hung colorful blankets and rows of strung peppers and onions. Saddles and horses' tack sat on the railing ledge, along with some fry pans and kettles. A ragged black boy was seated in the dust just outside Cummin's Station.

"Never rush right in," Gabe instructed. "Always be careful to size up the place. See what kind of people are hanging about."

Still in his Confederate uniform, he was concerned about Yankee soldiers who might not be as lenient toward him as Cochran was, in spite of the letter he had explaining our mission.

Then there were Indians. Some were harmless, others out to kill, especially anyone in a uniform. So we approached slowly from the back, where we dismounted our horses and hobbled them to the fence of the corral.

"You aimin' on telling them inside how we lost our boots?" Gabe asked me.

I saw that even asking the question made him uncomfortable and that was reward aplenty.

"No," I said. "I can't see how it's any of their business."

He nodded. "First thing we do is find out if that Yankee came through here with Sis Goose."

A hawk circled overhead as we headed toward the front entrance. Before we reached it, the little black boy came up and tugged Gabe's pants.

"Suh. I's hungry. Could you please give a coin to a little nigra boy like me?"

Gabe stopped and looked at him. "Don't you have a home?" he asked.

He shook his curly head. He was ragged and dirty, no shoes on his feet. "I comes from the Hardin place, over to the north. I ain't goin' back there, no suh, no."

"Did they free you?"

"Yassuh, but the war be over and those white peoples still all be killin' each other back there. No more shootin' fer this nigra boy. No suh. I seed 'nough of it."

"Shooting?" Gabe inquired.

"Yassuh. Them Yankees that come done shoot all the horses and dogs and wanna put the white folks outa the house. The white folks started shootin', and I run. Been runnin' ever since."

"How old are you?" Gabe asked.

"Doan rightly know, suh. I wuz born a little bit before the war. All I knows is, it was the summer of the bad rain."

Gabe nodded. "Means you're about nine. Come on inside and I'll buy you a bowl of beans and meat."

"Yassuh!"

The boy followed us into the cool inside of the station. Here were a few tables to sit down at, a stove on which was a large pot of what must have been the beans and meat, a bar, and a counter filled with merchandise.

Gabe sat the boy down at a table and ordered him a bowl of food and some cornbread. Then he asked about Sis Goose and the Yankee.

The man who owned the place, by the name of Max, ruminated a bit. "Come through here mebbe two days ago."

"How was the girl?" Gabe asked.

I held my breath. Would he say she was pregnant?

"Seemed aright."

"Did she seem like she wanted to be with him?"

"Nooo." Max shook his head. "He had her hands tied behind her back. Said she was wanted by the law. I mind my own business."

Gabe swore and asked if he knew where they were headed.

"Nearest law or Yankees be in San Felipe. He asked me the way."

Gabe thanked him and told me to find some boots. He found a pair as well, and while he was at it purchased some trousers, a shirt, and duster, too, the kind he'd had before the war when he rode the prairie for Pa.

"Tired of this damn uniform," he told Max. "I need a place to change."

Max showed him a curtain and he went behind it and put on his new clothes.

"You want me to get rid of the uniform?" Max asked.

"No. I'll keep it. Show it to my grandchildren someday," Gabe said.

When he paid, Max told him that the little boy had been loitering around and begging for two days. "He's got no place to go," Max finished.

Gabe nodded and without saying anything to me walked over to the table where the boy was wiping out his bowl with the last of his cornbread. "What's your name?" he asked.

"Hamilton. But everybody call me Ham."

"You intending on staying here and begging, Hamilton? Or would you like a home?"

I gasped. Gabe was going to bring him home!

The boy looked at him warily. "I still be free?"

"You'll always be free," Gabe told him. "But you still need to eat. And lay your head down someplace at night. Being free doesn't take care of that. Responsibility does. You have to learn to read and write. You want to do all that, come with me. I'll take you to a place where they'll teach you how."

It took only a minute for Ham to decide. "I come with you," he said, slipping off the chair. "Where we goin'?"

"A fine place," Gabe said. "I promise."

CHAPTER TWENTY-FOUR

THAT WAS the first glimmer I had into my brother's mind since he came home from the war. The way he was helping Ham, with all his own worries, Sis Goose being kidnapped, being commissioned to take over with the ranch, and me, Pa dying . . .

My mind couldn't get a purchase at first on why he was taking time to help Ham, and then I pondered it out.

Most likely he was trying to make up for those Indian women and children he'd killed. They, not Yankees, were his casualties of war. Ma had told me about them when she cautioned me to be patient with him.

Anyway, we fed and watered the horses and mule and then were on our way.

To San Felipe, Gabe said. "Even though I don't think Heffernan would be stopping at any Yankee headquarters or sheriff's office there. He's still a deserter. Though word may not have gotten out about him yet."

He put Ham on the horse behind him, and you could tell by the way the little boy clutched at his waist how scared he was. What did Gabe intend to do with him? Leave him? Where?

"I know some people in San Felipe," he said. "Catholic nuns. They take in children who have no one."

Catholic? We were Presbyterian. How did it come about that my brother knew Catholic nuns? There was more to him even, I decided, than met the eye. And then a frightening thought seized me. "You're not sending me to a Catholic school in New Orleans, are you?" I asked.

He grinned, enjoying my agony. "Should. Would do you a lot of good. But no, this is just a fine ladies' school, where you'll learn a lot more than embroidery, believe me. Officer I served with at Fort Belknap has his daughter there and told me all about it. You'll learn Latin and French, equations, philosophy. You'll quote Shakespeare and Cicero. Didn't do me any harm when I learned all that back in college in Virginia. You'll learn about the constellations in the sky and meet wellborn young men. You'll come home telling *me* what to do."

"I could do that now."

"You could try."

We covered ten miles that morning, and Gabe put his Indian training to work tracking a horse's footsteps on the sandy ground. Several times he got off his horse and examined the prints, pronouncing them to be made by a Yankee horse, which he could tell because of the horseshoe marks.

"You certainly are going slow there, Captain," I found myself saying to him. "If somebody I loved was kidnapped, I'd be racing across the prairie."

He gave me an odd look. "The sun getting to you, Luli? I've been tracking. When you track Indians you go steady and unrushed and sure of yourself."

I giggled. "So now Sis Goose is an Indian. Oh, look, there's something in the sand." I stopped and slid off my horse. "Signs, Gabe, the kind of signs Mercy Love makes when she spreads sand on her table at home. Come look."

He slipped off his horse and came over. He squatted down. "Where?"

"Right there. Can't you see? A moon and stars. A circle of stars. They say something about when we'll find her. And the moon is dripping blood. Oh, I wish I could understand what that means."

His face went hard. "There's no moon dripping blood there," he said sternly. He got up. "I see nothing. Now stop making a joke of this. There're no signs at all. Get back on your horse."

"But Gabe. You can't ignore such signs. The angels will get angry. You don't want to make the angels angry, do you?"

"Get back on your horse, Luli. Now."

"All right, if you want to be a spoilsport."

We went on. The horizon danced before my eyes. "Where are the mountains, Gabe? Where did they go?"

"No mountains here, Luli. We've passed them."

"You mean they passed us. They danced right by. Did you know that mountains can dance, Gabe?"

"Stop talking gibberish."

"Gibberish?" I got scared. I somehow sensed that the words coming out of my mouth were not just right, but I couldn't have stopped them coming out if somebody paid me new Yankee dollars. I closed my eyes and rocked to the rhythm of my horse's gait. I almost went to sleep. "Soon as Ma calls me I'm going in for the noon meal," I told him. "I hope she's got some of that good vegetable soup of hers. Wouldn't you like some of that vegetable soup, Gabe?"

"What I'd like is for you to shut your mouth for a while, dear sister," he said.

We soon reached a spring and Gabe told me to get off my horse, that we were all going to wash. I caught him looking at me out of the corner of his eyes. "We don't want to look like outriders to the nuns," he said. "Find someplace to wash and change your dress, Luli."

I was fishing out a clean dress from my saddlebags when I came across the blue cloak. "Who put this in here?" I asked.

"Pa suggested I bring 'em along," he said. "I've got Sis Goose's."

"But it's too warm. It must be over a hundred. I'm dying."

He looked at me in alarm. He lifted Ham off the horse and started toward me. "Pa said it was worth six bales of cotton just to see you two wearing these together."

"Pa just has a fancy for these cloaks, is all. Pa doesn't know the real world anymore. How could he? He hasn't been out of his bedroom in months."

"Don't bad-mouth Pa!"

"I'm sorry. But I'm never going to wear that cloak with Sis Goose again. Where is she? We'll never find her. She's gone from us. Flown away. Like geese do. Gone." Again the words were coming out of my mouth without my being able to control them. Lord, I hoped Gabe would remember his vow.

I threw my cloak on the dusty ground, an action I couldn't control.

"Pick it up, Luli."

"No." I was testing him. I almost ran to a place along the stream where I could have my privacy.

When I came back he and Ham were washed, too, and he was shaved and wearing a clean shirt.

My cloak was still on the ground. This was bad. A battle of wits between us was always bad. He was putting away his shaving gear. Ham was helping him.

"Get the cloak for me, Ham, would you?" he asked.

Ham picked it up. Gabe brushed it off and started toward me, putting it on my horse's back. I backed away.

"Stop it, Luli. No showdowns today."

I stopped.

He reached out one hand and I braced myself. "What's wrong with you?" I could hear the hurt in his voice. In a practiced way, like Ma did, he felt my face for fever. "You're burning up is what's wrong. God, child, you've got a first-rate fever. You've been talking crazier than a coot for the last hour."

"Gabe."

"What?"

"You've got angels on your shoulders. They're powerful pretty ones, too. And they like you, Gabe. They're going to help you."

His voice broke. "Ham, get me that large saddlebag in front, will you? There's a boy." He dug in it and brought out some boneset, Ma's remedy for fever. I hated the stuff but took it obediently because of all the trouble I'd been causing him. I saw Ma, not Gabe, standing over me now, cautioning me to behave.

Then I pointed out to Gabe how the sky was darkening in the west, ugly black clouds, and it was true, not some fancy I dreamed up. In the next instant I saw streaks of lightning, which always terrorized me, and I heard mutterings of thunder.

"Your horse," Gabe said.

"I know, I can't let him catch my fears, but I won't, don't worry."

I felt chilled, but I followed Gabe diligently, never holding him back. I don't know what we looked like coming into the lovely little town of San Felipe, but with it being near one o'clock and hot and everyone taking siesta and the storm threatening, no one was in the streets.

Gabe went right to the end of the dusty street where

there stood a Mexican-style church. Next to it was what appeared to be a convent, whitewashed and with pots of geraniums on the spacious front gallery, where there was also a settle and some chairs.

We got off the horses in front.

"Wait here," Gabe said.

Ham and I waited. My head was still throbbing. I wished Gabe would come out. I knew he was going to turn me over to the nuns for treatment, but I also knew he wouldn't leave until I was better.

Right now I'd be willing to have a tooth pulled to get out of here.

"You lucky you got such a brother to take care o' you," Ham said. "My brother wuz sold away."

Should I tell him now how such a brother could boss you around, scold you so you'd have to run to Mama, who'd send you right back to him again, maybe for more? No, this wasn't the time. Anyway, he'd been witness to some of it.

The door opened. Gabe came out. A nun was with him.

"As you can see, we're a little dusty for wear," he told her. "My ma would never let us in the house this way."

"Only thing I object to is the guns," she said. "You remember that, Gabriel. Leave them here at the door."

I felt naked without mine but minded how Gabe gave his over with no protest.

"Sister Geraldine, this is my little sister, Luanne. We

call her Luli. And this is Ham, the boy I told you about. Ham, take off your hat."

The boy did so.

"I'd like to go into all of it with you now, ma'am, but I'd be powerful appreciative if you'd have someone see first to my little sister. She's fearful ailing. I gave her some of Ma's boneset on the trail for fever, and I've got some laudanum, too." He pushed one of his saddlebags with his foot.

"Why, of course. Sister Helena!" she called out, then to us, "She's excellent with remedies. We'll put you right to bed. My, you are a pretty little girl."

"Be good, honey," Gabe winked at me, teasing, and hugged me, but I wouldn't let him go.

"Gabe, don't leave without me. Promise."

"Course not," he said with rough tenderness, which I recognized as his form of love.

I didn't know anything about nuns, so I at least expected Sister Helena to be as nice as the angels I'd seen on Gabe's shoulders. She was. She helped me into a soft nightdress and for some reason I felt no shame in front of her. She talked all the while. About my father, who they nursed back from the cholera years ago and who still sent around "tokens" of sides of meat, corn, flour, and wine, several times a year. About how Gabriel had been here a few years ago with Granville on a trip south.

By that time I was propped up against goose-down and feather pillows because somehow along the way I must have told her I had a terror of lightning storms and that Mama surrounded me with such pillows and quilts because God never let geese and chickens get struck by lightning.

Then, thanks to her magic remedies, which tasted a lot like Mercy Love's, I went to sleep and never woke until there was a gentle knock and the door opened so I could see both the sunshine and Gabe standing there.

"You up?"

I nodded.

"The sisters are at mass praying for my soul. Look, don't tell them you shot the colonel, will you? He was here with Sis Goose a few days ago and kind enough not to admit he was shot by a young girl."

"He was here?"

"Yes. Wanted a priest to marry them." He slumped against the doorjamb. "Thank God for Catholic rules. The priest wouldn't do it. Needed more time, he said. I'll wager he needed time to look into this colonel with the shot arm and a young, scared girl with him." He wasn't looking at me.

He gave the subject a new turn then. "Guess where I slept last night."

"In the barn with the horses."

"Do I smell that bad? No, I slept in the gallery, on the settle."

"Why?"

He shrugged. I could tell he just wanted to talk. And

if he raised his head, I wagered I would see his eyes full of tears again, brought on by talking of Sis Goose. "Army training," he said. "Always post watch. That way I was able to sleep with my gun. And I never got wet. Is your fever gone? You're not seeing any more angels?"

"They say you smell too bad."

He came into the room and pushed the hair off my face and felt my forehead. "Come on, get dressed then and come down for breakfast. We'll say our proper good-byes and get on with it."

At the door he stopped, turned, and examined his hat. "There's something you're not telling me about Sis Goose, isn't there?"

My mouth fell open.

"Look, I know you two have secrets. I know that's what girls do. But I hope it isn't something real important that you're keeping from me, Luli."

"I made her a promise not to tell, Gabe. And after we kept her freedom a secret from her for so long, it seemed the thing to do."

He nodded. "Yeah. But promises sometimes turn out to be trouble. Just like the promise I made to myself never to give you a good swat once in a while."

I was supposed to laugh. I didn't. He saw that and frowned.

"In it deep, are you?"

I nodded.

"Anybody going to get hurt?"

"Just hurt feelings," I said.

He sighed. "Well, if it's too much for you to handle you can come to me. You know that. You can come to me for anything."

Did he have to be so nice? By all that was holy, why did I make that promise to Sis Goose not to tell him she was carrying his child?

"Come on now, get dressed," he said. "I'm about starved."

CHAPTER TWENTY-FIVE

WHEN WE LEFT, Sister Geraldine gave us some sliced baked ham on thick slices of freshly made bread. She gave me a stone jar of tea. "It will keep hot at least until noon," she said. "And it's good for you."

Whatever arrangements she and Gabe made about Ham I didn't know. But I know that Gabe did give her money to clothe the boy and get him a good pair of shoes.

She said she would pray for us. I somehow had the feeling we'd need it.

SISTER GERALDINE had told Gabe that Colonel Heffernan said he was going to cross the river and head for Matagorda, near the Gulf.

"I dressed his shoulder while he was here," she said. "The wound is superficial."

"Lucky you," Gabe told me when we were on our way again. "I'll have to tell Cochran that you didn't kill him."

We had to cross the river to find Heffernan, and so we rode to the riverside where there was a ferry.

The man who operated it lived in a log cabin on a small nearby hill. "Yell for a crossing," a crudely painted sign read.

"I done yelled," a voice said. "An' he said he be comin' soon. Waited for freedom, guess we kin wait for him."

Under a grove of trees just to the left of us they were, and we hadn't seen them. A group of negroes with some worn-down mules carrying their few possessions. Gabe said hello and asked them where they were going.

They looked the worse for wear, like they'd stayed out all night in the hard rain. There were five of them: two women, two men, and one young boy. They came forward.

"I's Felix," the one who'd spoken to us said. He was gray-haired and strong looking, though obviously not young. His eyes were like the eyes of Mercy Love's owl, seeing everything and giving back nothing.

"Gabe Holcomb and my sister Luli," Gabe said.

The man nodded. "This here's my son Charley, brother Knox, an' Sis Eda and Sis Hannah. We been travelin' for days. Goin' south to look for work. Done left Marse Jones for good," he finished.

Gabe nodded. "Where you from?"

"Up north a ways. Fifteen miles above Washington. My wife, she dead. Beaten to death by Massa's driver. She wuz carryin' another chile. Man dug a hole in the ground, made her lay face down in it, and beat her till she died. That wuz two years ago now."

Gabe nodded. “Sorry about that. I’ve traveled a bit up that way and heard that old man Jones was rough on his people.”

“Rough don’t say it,” Felix answered. “That man made us wear chains sometimes when we worked in the fields. He had sixty bloodhounds that he rented out to slave catchers. My brother Horace, he done run off this May after we hear the war may be over. Massa ask for his return in paper. Willin’ to give money. Next thing we know that Granger fella down in Galveston say we all be free.”

Gabe nodded. “Granger is the commander of the District of Texas. That was Order Number Three.”

“At first,” Felix went on, “we all jumpin’ up an’ down. Feel like heroes, ’cause we lived to see freedom. Then Massa ask us to work for him. Nobody stayed. An’ so we been travelin’. Now we outa food and have no money and doan know what to do.”

“Ate nuthin’ but berries and grapes for five days,” his son Charley put in.

“Let’s get to the other side of the river first,” Gabe said. “I can give you some supplies.”

THE FERRY MAN came down the hill. The ferry looked like an oversized raft with rickety railings on the sides, but he said it could fit all of us. “It’ll cost you five dollars,” he said to Gabe. Then he looked at the crowd of negroes. “You got any money?”

“No, suh,” said Felix.

"I'll pay for them," Gabe offered.

And I was close enough to him this time to see his money. Again it was Yankee, not Confederate. More of Pa's money.

I supposed Pa had made some sort of bargain with the group of important men he knew and had enough Yankee dollars now to replace his Confederate money. But what did people do who didn't have a pa like that, I wondered. I must ask Gabe.

I heard him talking to the river man about Heffernan. "Yeah, he come this way, last night afore the rain," the man said. "Pretty little girl he had with him, but I got the feelin' they weren't hitched. She didn't even talk to him."

Although the river was somewhat swollen by last night's rains, the trip across was uneventful. I held on to my horse's reins to steady myself. And to steady her. Gabe did the same with his horse. Of course the mule was as steady as a rock with all the supplies it was carrying.

On the other side we stepped onto a wharf and once on steady ground again, Gabe began to go through the contents of the bags the mule was carrying.

He gave the freedmen a goodly piece of bacon, some corn, and flour, and directed them to a plantation nearby where they could work for wages.

"Why do you give away so much?" I asked him as we continued on.

He didn't answer for a moment and then, like Rooney

Lee, he told me. "There shouldn't be any split in this country, Luli. We're all one country. Pa and Granville and I were never for secession. But we fought for Texas, Granville and I. And only lately, with this business with Sis Goose, do I realize how we've wronged the negroes. It's going to take a long time to get back on our feet again, but we can make up for some of it along the way."

It was the longest speech I'd ever heard him make.

"Pa never mistreated his negroes," I said.

"Slavery is mistreatment. Look what I've done to Sis Goose. But to talk that way during the war could earn you a hangman's rope around here. And we're, none of us, prepared in any way, for running our places without the negroes. I'm thinking of hiring some Scottish laborers. I hear they are hard workers. Because, in time, our negroes will drift off. Look, up ahead, does that seem like a town to you?"

I peered over what seemed like miles of wildflowers and did see some building in the distance against the hard blue sky. "Yes."

"It must be Fort Chivatato. The fort's long abandoned, but there is still supposed to be a sort of town there."

As we got closer we could see the dilapidated buildings huddled against the endless Texas sky. There were about four places of business and six homes. One house was larger, with a two-story balcony that didn't look strong enough to stand on, and windows that gaped at you.

When we got closer we could see a sign banging in a sudden wind that seemed to blow through the forlorn town. BOARDINGHOUSE, it read.

Outside several horses were hobbled. One had USA branded on its rump and sported a saddle blanket of blue that said the same thing in gold letters.

In the background, about half a mile away, loomed the old log fort. Deserted.

"They're here," Gabe said.

He retreated a little to a nearby grove of cottonwood trees and I followed. "We'll just wait here a bit. He's planning to go somewhere. Else the horse would be in back in the barn."

So we waited. We got off our horses and crouched behind the tree trunks. Gabe had his rifle at the ready and so I took mine from its sling on my saddle and cradled it in my arms. Bees droned and up ahead in the town a man crossed the street where suddenly rolls of tumbleweed were blowing and dust was picking up. He had an old hound dog at his heels. He went into a building with a sign that read SALOON, and the dog waited outside on the wooden walk.

In a little while the front door of the boardinghouse opened and a man came out.

Heffernan. Still in his Yankee uniform, though it and his boots looked hard worn.

He stood there, lighted a cheroot, and cupped the

light with his hands. Then he took a deep draught and continued standing there, looking around.

"Hold still," Gabe cautioned.

Then Heffernan went back to the front door, held it open, and stood talking with someone. "Half an hour." The wind carried the words to us as if they were in a tunnel.

He got on his horse and rode down to the end of the street, where he went into the saloon.

Gabe got up. "Get that blue cloak of yours out," he said to me.

I stared at him as if he had taken leave of his senses.

"Go on, do as I say."

I searched clumsily in the saddlebag until I found the blue velvet cloak. "Put it on," Gabe directed. "You're going inside and you're going to find Sis Goose. I'll stay out here in case he comes back sooner than half an hour."

I put the cloak on, not wanting to argue with him. At this moment he brooked no argument. "I'll look like a butterfly in a grave, wearing this in there," I told him.

He paid me no mind. Just got up and adjusted the cloak around me and clasped it at the neck. "I want you to look like that to Sis Goose. Here," and he fished in his saddlebag and brought out hers, shook it out, and gave it to me. "Give it to her."

"What do I say to her if she's in there?" I asked.

"Ask her to come out. Tell her I'll handle Heffernan, not to worry. Ask her if she'll come home with us. Do I have to tell you what to say? You're the one who has secrets with her. She's been like a sister to you since you were born. Now leave your gun." He took it. "You've got about twenty-five minutes."

"Wouldn't it be better if you went, Gabe?"

"No." His face was like a mask. "She's mad as hell at me for not telling her she was free. I'd need an hour to convince her otherwise. You go ahead. And give her the cloak. It'll remind her of things. Go on now."

He spoke to me as if I were ten years old. But I went. Across the dusty ground, up the steps to the boarding-house, and then through the door. I didn't bother to knock.

CHAPTER TWENTY-SIX

INSIDE THE front room was a desk, behind which a grizzly old man stood. "You want something, Missy?" he asked. "We got rooms, nice enough."

"No. I'm looking for Rose Smith. A young woman who—"

"Doan have no Rose Smith registered."

"She's with Colonel Heffernan." I near choked on the name.

"Oh, that one. Room 3D. You say you are?"

"Didn't say, but she's my sister."

"Go on up the stairs. Right at the end of the hallway."

I hurried up. Twenty-five minutes, Gabe had said. How long would it take to convince Sis Goose to come with me? Would I have to convince her? I made swift time down the hallway. Some of the doors were not marked, but there, at the end, was the room. It said 3D, but the D was hanging half off. The woodwork was dark, and although it was a bright day outside none of the brightness seemed to come in the one window at the end of the hall.

I clutched her blue velvet cloak against my breast and knocked on the door. Softly. There were footsteps inside and it opened a crack.

Through that crack I saw her familiar beautiful brown eyes, saw them go wide, heard her gasp, "Luli!"

The door creaked as it opened. I just stood there and she reached out for me and hugged me as if we'd never been parted. "Luli, what are you doing here? How did you find me?"

And then it came to her. "Gabe?"

"He's downstairs. Outside, Sis. We came after you. We saw Heffernan go into the saloon down the street. We know we have only half an hour."

"The saloon, yes. If he's there, it'll be more than half an hour. He told me he was going to see the old fort. Oh, Luli, why did you come?"

She almost wailed it. Sorrowfully.

"To bring you home. Come on now, there's no time for questions. Get your things together. And here." I held out the blue cloak. "Remember this? Gabe would like you to wear it."

She whirled on me. Her eyes blazed. "Gabe! Does he think he still has the right to tell me what to do? I'm free now, and I'm not a little girl any longer."

It took me by surprise, much as I feared it would happen. "Gabe loves you, Sis. He wants to get you away from Heffernan."

She put the cloak around her shoulders in front of a

dirty mirror. The room had a bed and a nightstand and a slop bucket. No rugs on the floor. Tattered lace curtains on the windows. I shuddered.

"Thank you for bringing this. Tell Mama that it'll help cover my delicate condition. Remember we used to play at one of us being in a delicate condition?"

"Yes, I remember." She showed, even with the cape on. Oh, what would I say to Gabe when she came down?

"How we laughed! Well, I can tell you, Luli, it's nothing to laugh about. I'm carrying a baby, a real live baby." Tears were in her eyes, and she drew the blue cloak over her tummy.

"Gabe's baby," I reminded her.

"Did you ever tell him?"

"No."

She gasped. "Why?" She turned to me.

"Because I kept my promise to you. I owed you that."

"And nobody else knows, either?"

"No."

"My God. What would they all say?"

"It's up to you to tell them, Sis. You wanted it that way."

"My mother died having me. Do you think I'll die, Luli?"

"No. Not if you come home with us and are properly cared for. Mama will get you a doctor."

"The colonel says he knows how to deliver babies. Learned it in the army. Says he's going to take care of me, Luli."

"Why would you want to go with him?"

She turned to me. "He gave me freedom."

"Then why did everyone we meet on the way here tell us you acted as if you didn't want to be with him? One person said he had your hands tied."

She looked out the window. "I can't go back with you and Gabe, even if I wanted to. Heffernan says if I run off, he'll find me and kill me. And my child. I don't care for myself, Luli. But I care for my baby. Maybe with the third generation it'll have some luck in the world."

"Gabe will protect you," I promised. "Always."

"Oh?" She turned on me. "The way he protected me from the truth of my being free?"

"Sis, I did, too. We had to. And so did Mama and Pa. And you know how they love you."

"But Gabe's love was supposed to be different." Tears came down her face and her chest heaved. She wiped her face with her hand. "Why didn't he come up instead of sending you? Sent you to do his dirty work for him."

"Sis." I took a step toward her. "Because he saw Heffernan leave. Heard him say he'd be back in half an hour. Because he's waiting for him. Come on, Sis, you can't pretend that you don't love Gabe. I know you. I know you do."

"Of course I do! I love him and I hate him for what he did to me. But if it wasn't for Heffernan's threat to kill me, at least I'd go down and give Gabe what-for. Then I'd think about forgiving him. Now that isn't possible."

"Oh, Sis, come on with me, please. We can work all these other things out. Gabe loves you so much that I think he'll die if you don't come with us. And I want you, too. We all do. You know, Pa is dying. And he wants to see you again."

That struck her. "Pa? Dying?"

"Yes. He's going fast, too. Likely he's lying there in his bed right now just waiting to see you first before he dies."

I was being unfair, I knew it. But I had to use everything I had.

She bit her lower lip and dropped her eyes. "You'd better go. He may be back any minute."

"I . . . can't . . . go, Sis. Not without you."

"You want Heffernan to shoot Gabe? He will, you know. He's crazy enough. And he'll shoot you, too. So go."

"What'll I tell Gabe?"

"Oh God. Tell him I love him. Tell him anything. That if he loves me and doesn't want me to be killed, he'll leave. That he'll find someone else. Explain things to Pa and Mama. Tell them I'm sorry."

She was ushering me from the room as she spoke. I was at the door. I took one last look at her. "I can shoot a gun, you know. And if you think Gabe is going to just leave on your say-so, then you're crazy, too."

She hugged me. "I'm going to keep the cloak, Luli. Thank you. Thank Gabe for coming. Tell him I'm happy."

"You're carrying his child!"

"Go, Luli, go. And don't ever run off with a scoundrel."

CHAPTER TWENTY-SEVEN

I WENT SWIFTLY downstairs and out the door. I looked up the street. Far at the end I saw a figure on horseback, talking with some other Yankee soldiers who were likely visiting the town. Heffernan!

"Luli, come quick," Gabe called softly.

I scooted to him under the cottonwood trees.

"He's coming back," Gabe said in a harsh whisper. "Where is she? Where's Sis?"

"She . . . won't . . . come . . . down. I'm sorry, Gabe. I did my best."

"Still sees me as the master and her as the slave, is that it? Else Heffernan has got her seeing things that way."

"She said she loves you and she hates you. She said, too, that Heffernan would track her down and kill her if she left him for you."

Something inside me wouldn't let me tell him about the baby. Even now. Especially now, because he'd go crazy if he knew.

"Well, he's going to have to get past me to do it."

I picked up my rifle and cocked it. "I'll help you. Tell me what to do."

"Just watch my back. I'm going to demand he bring her down and hand her over. After all, he kidnapped her when he deserted."

"Gabe, there are other Yankee soldiers in the saloon."

"Just a gang having a last drink before they go home. They don't want a fight any more than Ma does. If he kills me," and he turned to look at me, "don't stay around. Get on your horse and go. Take my horse, too, and go back to the nuns in San Felipe. Write to Ma and she'll send someone to escort you home. You've got to promise me."

I promised him.

It took forever for Heffernan to reach the boardinghouse. I could hear my heart beating. What was that other noise? Gabe's? Who was that behind the tattered lace curtain on the second floor? It was room 3D, I was sure of it. The curtains parted, and then someone was wiping the dust off the windows with a hand.

That someone was still wearing the blue cloak, I could see. And I thought, crazily, again, that if she came downstairs onto the porch with Heffernan, Gabe would see she was carrying a child.

Heffernan finally reached the boardinghouse, dismounted his horse, and without looking around started up the steps.

Two things happened then: Sis Goose came clattering

down the steps and appeared on the porch, and Gabe stood up in full view and said, "Hold it right there, Heffernan."

"Who the hell are you?" Heffernan asked, pulling out his own revolver. And I was reminded that he'd never met Gabe before.

"It's Gabe," we heard Sis tell him. "I think he's come for me."

"Gabe, is it? Oh, so this is the massa's son who didn't even have to go down to the quarters at night to get what he wanted. Who had it right in his own house. This is the massa's son who's been at you till he got you pregnant. Show him how far gone you are, Sis Goose," and he unlatched the cloak and pulled it off from her.

And there, in the light of God's good day, you could see her rounded belly.

"You see that, Gabe?" Heffernan yelled. "There's what you did and I'm willing to care for."

"Noooo," Gabe yelled and leaned over his rifle and aimed at Heffernan. But Heffernan fired first. The shot was loud and seemed to echo right through town and bounce off the old boards of buildings and bring out the people.

Gabe doubled over and clutched himself, and I thought, *Oh God, dear God, don't let him be hurt bad.*

I went to him and leaned over him. "Gabe?"

"It's my shoulder. But I can get one shot in."

"Let me do it."

"I have to try, Luli. You have to let me."

He stood up and Heffernan waited, laughing.

"Gabe, don't," Sis Goose begged.

"Move out of the way, Sis," he said.

She moved, a big answer to him on her part, and Gabe fired but missed. Between his bleeding shoulder and the knowledge of Sis Goose carrying his child, he was completely undone.

He slumped down. "He's all yours, hon," he said to me. "Give it your best. Remember what we taught you."

I stood up and took aim.

Heffernan laughed. "So he sends his little sister to do his fighting for him now."

"She's good," Sis Goose said. She'd moved back to Heffernan.

"I'm wearin' proof of it," he said. "This little witch is crazy."

"Move, Sis," I barked at her. A hundred words I wanted to say, but that was all that was good for now.

"Don't, Luli, please. Don't you remember?" she asked.

"I don't because you don't. You use your memories and hopes to play people, so I don't, now move."

Heffernan pushed her away and aimed at me. No going back now. I aimed true, steady, unafraid, as I'd been taught. Then I fired.

Just as I took aim, or some second in eternity afterward, Heffernan pulled Sis Goose toward him. More in front of him, to be exact.

There. In that spot where the heart is.

This time the shot didn't ring out. This time there was a deathly thud and it stopped, right in the center of Sis Goose's forehead.

She took the shot for him. Not because she wanted to but because he wanted her to. She took it and crumpled right at his feet.

Sis Goose was dead. I screamed. I remember screaming and screaming, and I remember Gabe crawling over to me, and with one arm around me saying, "Stop it, Luli, stop it!" All half delirious-like. And then, raising his head to look at the porch of the boardinghouse, and saying, "Oh my God, what's happened? Oh my God!"

And then I do not remember any more. At all.

CHAPTER TWENTY-EIGHT

HERE IS WHAT they told me happened next.

There were people in the town after all. Half a dozen of them came running on hearing the gunshots. And those soldiers came who were on their way home.

All of them still very much officers, one of them a doctor, like the whole thing had been planned by the gods. First they had to decide who was in charge. Then they had to see to Sis Goose, but before they could do that they had to pull her away from Gabe. He was sitting on the porch, rocking her back and forth in his arms.

"She's dead," one of them told Gabe as they gently pried his hands loose. "Son, she's dead." Turned out he was the doctor. "You have to let her go, son."

Dead. Free, finally. Sis Goose was free. And I wondered what things would have been like if the Texas plantation owners had told their slaves they were free over two years now. There would be no Heffernan at our place. There would be no Sis Goose dead.

"And that blood on your shirt isn't all hers," the doctor

went on kindly. "Come on, son. It's yours. You're shot. Let's see to it."

"Only if you bring her along," Gabe muttered. "I'll not let her go."

They promised they would see to her only because Gabe wouldn't release her. We all, Heffernan included, were escorted to the saloon.

It seems the saloon was the most decent place they had in town. There everything was polished and clean. The doctor went ahead to prepare a settle in his "surgery," a back room where he'd already treated some townspeople. The officer who carried Sis Goose back set her down on a settle and covered her with a blanket.

"Who shot her?" asked Major Cogan, the officer in charge.

I wanted to speak. I wanted to tell them it was me. But I couldn't. Some force, some hand, had reached out of the heavens to strangle me after that first scream when I saw Sis Goose crumple to the ground. I plunged into a whirlwind of silence, as if into a creek of warm water that was now up to my neck. And I didn't want to get out.

Gabe said, "He shot at us first. He hit me and I went down. My sister picked up her gun to defend us. He was aiming to shoot her. And the moment she fired he—he pulled Sis in front of him. That's what we call her. Sis Goose. Her real name is Rose Smith."

Major Cogan looked at me. He was not tall by any means, but there was an air of command about him. He was young, too, with long sideburns and a pointed beard on his chin. "Is that the way it happened?" he asked.

I nodded.

"Can't you say 'yes, sir'? Can't you talk?"

"She's my little sister," Gabe said, as if that should explain it all. He was clutching his shoulder and there was blood all over his hand.

"Why you dragging her around like this?"

"I'm her guardian."

"Still doesn't explain."

"We come from our ranch up near Washington. It's occupied by your people. I was given permission by a Captain Cochran up there to make this trip to bring back Sis Goose. I needed my sister along. This note explains that Heffernan is a deserter." He pulled Cochran's paper out of his pocket. It had some blood on it. "I just got discharged myself."

Major Cogan read it, nodded his head, and gave it back.

"Been killing Yankees?" one man asked.

Gabe shook his head. "Would have if I was ordered to. But I was guarding the frontier from Indians. Fort Belknap. Name's Captain Holcomb."

"Give the captain the respect he deserves," Cogan chided his men. "Could your sister talk before the shooting?"

Gabe nodded, wincing in pain. "Like a magpie. Never shut up. Never let me off the hook."

"Let's get that arm fixed," the captain-doctor said. "And I want to take a look at your sister, too."

So I sat in the captain-doctor's surgery while he cut off Gabe's torn and bloody shirt, examined the wound, and pronounced that there were no shattered bones, no bullet lodged in there, and that it was just a nasty flesh wound. He washed the hurt place and dusted it with morphine. He bandaged it up and gave Gabe some rum and laudanum for the pain.

I just sat there, watching and crying without making a sound. Tears kept pouring down my face. Then Gabe asked me to go out to his horse and get a clean shirt out of his saddlebags. It was the first time he'd spoken to me since the shooting. I was never so glad to do anything. I knew he and the doctor were going to talk about me, but I didn't care. Gabe had spoken to me, and that was all that mattered.

When I got back the doctor helped Gabe into the shirt and then came over to see to me. He felt my pulse. Then he took a peculiar-looking instrument out of his pocket, put one end in either ear and another against the top of my dress, right about where my heart should be. "Don't be afraid," he said. "It's called a stethoscope. Been around since 1838 but few, if any, of my colleagues use it. It's my little secret. It lets me listen to your heart."

He looked into both my eyes and made me open my mouth. He felt me around my neck. "You feeling all right otherwise?" he asked.

I nodded yes.

"You're in shock," he told me and Gabe. "You've got a pallor, cold and clammy skin, and a weak pulse. You allowed to have brandy?"

I looked at Gabe, who nodded yes. So the doctor poured a small glass and I drank it. Vile stuff.

Gabe slid off Doctor Tucker's table, for that was the good doctor's name, and the doctor said I should lie down on a small bed in the surgery. So I did. He covered me. I closed my eyes, but all I could see was Sis Goose in that blue velvet cloak, being pulled in front of Heffernan, then sliding to the ground. I saw the bloody wound on her forehead, heard my gun go off, over and over, until the sound of it, and the brandy, put me out.

TWO THINGS of immense importance happened in the next few days.

We buried Sis Goose in the small cemetery on a hill outside town. Gabe didn't want to. He wanted to take her home. But Major Cogan and Captain-Doctor Tucker advised against it. Too far away, they said. Too hot. He couldn't manage with that arm of his. Not a good idea. Why, he was running a fever. As a matter of fact, he and I shouldn't go any farther than San Felipe and the good nuns for a while. We should stay there until we were both better.

What they didn't know is that it would take years for us both to get better. Or maybe they did know and just didn't say.

Gabe was hurting, and not only in his shoulder. He walked around like a man in a daze. He was broken in places that had never been pierced by a bullet.

The doctor kept giving him medicine for the fever.

And I, I was just broken in half. Half of me knew it would be my responsibility to get Gabe to San Felipe, to the nuns, where they would help his physical wounds, even as they had helped Pa mend. And the other half of me wanted to be buried with Sis Goose.

We buried her in her blue velvet cloak.

I cried more silent tears at the funeral. And Gabe made no attempt to comfort me. Standing there on that small hill, he looked like some ghost out of a Dickens novel, with his duster flapping in the wind.

Would the arm mend properly?

Alone with Doctor Tucker, who asked to see me after the funeral, I wrote it on a piece of paper, because I still couldn't speak.

"Yes," he said. "You must give him time."

"But he's got to run the ranch when we get home. And my pa is dying," I wrote.

"Half the country is hurting like you two are," Doctor Tucker told me. "The war has left its toll. Some men are doing without arms or legs. Lord knows I amputated enough of them. Some are blind or addicted to painkillers. We all just have to go on. Now what else is bothering you? Tell me?"

I blushed and wrote it down. After all, he was a doctor. "I missed my woman's time of the month," I wrote. "How can that be?"

"Too much anxiety," he said. "And with all of this, with your being in shock and unable to speak, it may not come until you settle down again. Just try to forgive yourself for shooting the girl. From what your brother tells me, it wasn't your fault."

I wrote again. "Did he say that?"

"Yes."

More writing. "But I think he hates me."

"He doesn't," Tucker said. "He's got his own self to hate, from what he tells me, for not telling her she was free for over two years. Tell me one more thing: Does he treat you all right? Your brother?"

"What do you mean?" I wrote. "We fight sometimes. Sometimes I win, sometimes he does. Is that what you mean?"

"Never mind. You just answered my question."

The other thing that happened was that we had an inquest for Sis Goose's death.

Then and there, in the saloon after the funeral. Major Cogan said we should really go to New Orleans for it, but since Gabe and I weren't fit to travel, we'd have it now.

Heffernan was present and testifying.

They put me on the stand, which was a bar stool, and I considered it no fitter place. I had to write my answers. And then they put Gabe there, and he spoke shakily and told them how it had truly happened. How we were defending ourselves after Heffernan shot, and I did not set out to kill Sis Goose.

"Did you intend to kill Colonel Heffernan?"

"Yes," I wrote. "He was intending to kill me. It was self-defense."

They dismissed the charges against me and Gabe. We were free to go, as free as either of us ever would be. Heffernan they took in hand because he still had to face a court-martial.

We left for San Felipe two days later. I still couldn't talk. Gabe talked at me, not to me, telling me to ready for the trip back.

They bade us good-bye. Doctor Tucker spoke quietly and separately to us both before we left. I don't know what he told Gabe, but he spoke to him like Pa would.

"Take care of your brother," he told me. "Be good to him. It's your responsibility now to shoot the snakes and the wild boar if you meet any. He said you're capable and smart."

I warmed at the words. And I hugged Doctor Tucker before we left. He said any day now something could happen to shock me back into speaking again. I wanted to believe him.

CHAPTER TWENTY-NINE

I SHOT ONE rattlesnake on the way back. It slithered into our camp that night. I had gathered the wood for the fire and rubbed the steel and flint together to start it. I cooked the supper and cleaned up afterward.

Gabe spoke to me, giving directions. We would take our watches, as usual, he said. If he saw something, he'd wake me so I could ready my gun. There was no more talk about "others out here like us" because he knew there never could be. And no more talk about who was scared and who wasn't because I knew now that I would be scared, too, just sitting down in Ma's house.

He saw the rattlesnake first. I picked up my gun, feeling it an alien thing in my hands. I sat there just looking at it dumbly.

"Come on, shoot!" he urged.

I shot. I killed the rattlesnake. Just like I had killed Sis Goose.

"It only took you a hundred years!" he scolded. Raw, unconcealed anger. I turned away and he picked up the snake and threw it into the far night.

I took the first watch. There were no stars in the sky.

THE NEXT day we reached San Felipe and the Sisters of Charity.

They welcomed us. They exclaimed over Gabe's wound and took him in hand and changed the bandages. He told them what had happened and how I couldn't talk. And Sister Geraldine took me in her arms and called me poor child and hugged me.

We saw Ham. And the reunion was joyful between him and Gabe, the way it used to be with me. I know Sister Geraldine spoke to Gabe in private about me. I know she told him I was hurting because he hadn't spoken like his old self to me.

I know this because I wrote it out for her in one of our conversations.

We sat at table together. We enjoyed Ham's company and the food and the talk, and still Gabe never teased or joked with me.

I went to take a siesta that last afternoon of our stay because I was tired, because tomorrow morning we were leaving for home, and because I needed to think. About Mama and what I would tell her about Sis Goose. About Pa and what he would say to me. Would they ever forgive me?

I suppose I could have gone into the chapel, like Sister suggested. I tried. I did try.

But when I opened the heavy, dark door I nearly wet my pants.

There was Gabe. Seated in the third row from the back, his hat off. Just sitting there, doing nothing. Still, the idea of my strong, Indian-fighting brother, my shot-up, bandaged-up brother even coming in here . . .

I closed the door and crept upstairs to my room to rest.

As long as I live I'll never forget that image of him sitting there and praying. Because that's what he was doing. Why else does a person go to a place like that with all those statues staring at you?

And as long as I live I'll never tell him I saw him there, either.

But never mind Gabe. What about me?

For no matter what anyone said to me, even with Gabe testifying that it was not my fault, even with Major Cogan setting us free of all charges, even with Sister Geraldine talking softly to me and tucking me in and telling me that God did not hold me accountable, even with all that, I did not feel forgiven.

It wasn't God that I needed to forgive me.

Afternoon sunlight filtered in through the blinds. From somewhere downstairs a nun was playing a harp. The song was "Greensleeves." I fell asleep. I don't know how long.

It was then that I heard some men talking. I looked out the window to the barnyard and I saw Gabe and Priam, the nuns' man-about-the-place.

Priam was checking the cinch on Gabe's saddle.

Gabe was saddled up! He was leaving! Without me! How, oh how, had this come about? *He was leaving me here with the nuns!*

How could he get home alone? Who would do for him? Who would gather wood for his fire? Strike the steel and flint to start it? Shoot the rattlesnakes?

Just because I'd frozen before shooting that rattlesnake around our fire, had he given up on me? And then I saw Ham on a horse. Not mine, but one belonging to the nuns.

Oh, he was taking Ham and not me! I stumbled about, looking for a robe and my moccasins. I opened the door and fumbled my way down the stairs.

I ran through the house and out the back door. Over the back verandah and out to the barnyard.

They were gone!

I ran down the path on the side of the house that led to the street. They were in the street already. Several houses away.

I stood there like a jackass in the rain. And then, not thinking, I called out.

"Gabe! Gabriel Holcomb, you come back here!"

They stopped. They turned their horses to look at me and I ran to them, running until I was out of breath. I stood in front of them in the afternoon street. Oh, I could see their faces all right. And they could see mine.

"Gabriel Holcomb," I scolded, just like Mama would

when he came into the house with muddy boots. "Where do you think you're going?"

He scowled. Then he shook his head. "You're talking," he said.

"I'm doing more than talking. I'm giving you the what-for you deserve. Where do you think you're going without me? Who's going to light your fire, cook your food, kill your rattlesnakes? Ham? You know you need me. Do you hear me?"

"The whole town does."

"And why would you leave me here? What for?"

"Leave you? Do I look like I'm leaving you? Where are my saddlebags? Where's the mule? You're really teched in the head now. Besides which you look really domineering in your robe and slippers in the middle of the street."

I looked down at myself in horror and hugged myself for modesty.

"Where are you going then?" I demanded.

"Taking one of the horses to have its shoe repaired at the blacksmith at the end of the street. Is that all right with you, madam?"

He was joking with me again. It was so all right with me I wanted to pick up stones and weeds and throw them, cry out, and do other necessary solemn acts, like Grandpa had done when he claimed the land, only I didn't know what they were.

"All right if we go get the horse's shoes fixed now?" he asked.

I nodded. "Be back in time for supper. We ride tomorrow morning."

"There's one thing you're forgetting, Luli. I've got to come back with you. Can't leave you here. I promised Cochran. You're under my recognizance, remember? That's his language for it. In mine it's Southern honor."

I just looked at him. It meant a lot to him, that honor business.

"It's what the war was all about, Luli. Lost or not. It's what we're all about, and if I have to teach you that, I will. Anyway, glad you're talking."

"Me, too."

"Remember, no sass."

"No sass," I agreed.

I turned and started walking back to the convent.

EPILOGUE

YOU WOULD think things were all right after that. They were, in small portions, like a spoon of sugar in a lifetime's cup of coffee. We had more bitter than sweet between us. And because of that we trod like the ground was full of rattlesnakes that I couldn't shoot in a hundred years.

I sit here in my room of the log house, the same room Pa had when he was alive, and I have my after-school cup of tea and write in my diary. Bone weary I am and only twenty-one years of age.

I have been teaching school here now for what seems like years. I teach the freedmen's children. It's a promise Pa made to them that 19th of June when he gave them their freedom so many years ago, and an obligation we have. The freedmen call the day Juneteenth now and have a great celebration.

I teach eight children. I could do more.

Pa died the summer Gabe and I came home from our trip. He did not take it well that Sis Goose was dead.

Gabe wanted to spare him and me by telling him that Heffernan shot her.

But I said, "Please, Gabe," because I don't sass him anymore, "please let me tell him the truth."

He looked hesitant.

"Pa always liked the truth," I reminded him. "It's about Southern honor."

He just looked at me with a strange light in his eyes and said, "Go ahead."

And so I did. Did I say it was easy? Pa lay in bed and cried. Gabe looked away, out the window. I wiped Pa's eyes. "My poor little Goose Girl," he said, "and carrying a child, too. My first grandchild. Yours, Gabe. You sure you tried your best to get her back?"

"Yes, sir." Gabe's answer covered a whole range of emotions.

Then Pa said, "My poor Luli. What a way to have to grow up."

Within a week he died. We buried him in the family cemetery.

Now Ma was something else. She took us both into the kitchen and gave us what-for. Couldn't we have done this? And why didn't we think of that? If both of us were just a bit younger she'd whip us with a broom handle. The two of us, the best shots in the county, and we couldn't put a bullet between that man's eyes? "What happened to you, Gabe, when you took that first shot?"

"I didn't . . . ," he answered, "you know . . ."

"No, I don't. Why don't you tell me."

"I didn't know she was carrying my child, Ma. The idea threw me like the best bronco in the corral."

She looked at me. "I know you didn't tell me. You didn't tell him, either?"

I shrank into the floor. I told her no. And to her why, oh to her why I said I thought it was Sis Goose's place to tell him.

For the first time in my life Ma slapped me. On the face. Even Gabe winced and tried to protect me. "She had my back in the gunfight, Ma. C'mon, she's had a rough time."

"She wouldn't have had to have your back if she'd properly prepared you for what was coming. Playing games is what she was doing."

"Come on, Ma. Jeez. You don't know what she's been through. I can't allow you to treat her like this."

Mama's eyes popped. "You can't allow . . . you . . . can't allow . . ."

Gabe worked his charm then, and he had plenty of it. He put his arm around Ma's shoulders. "You gonna kick me out?" he asked her. "Hey? Where do I go next? The barn?"

She broke then as he knew she would. She cried against his broad chest, and he held her while she cried it out. He signaled me with his head to leave the room for now, and so I went upstairs to my room.

He came upstairs in a little bit. I heard him talking

softly to Ma, bringing her along, settling her in her room. Then he came to mine and closed the door. "I'm sorry about all that," he said.

"Thanks for defending me."

"It's part of what I do. I wasn't fast enough this time." He came over to my bed, where I was sitting looking through some pictures. He put a hand under my chin and turned my face toward him. "Wow. You better get down to Mercy Love's and get some remedy for that. It's starting to swell."

I nodded.

"Ma will get over it. It's just her way of responding to the news."

"All we need is for us to get over it," I told him.

He sighed. "You're doing good, Luli. You're recovering."

It is taking time, lots of time, but I am recovering. Don't I go once a week to our cemetery to lay flowers on Pa's grave? Didn't I greet Granville when he came home, all properlike? Didn't I take part in Christmas like I wasn't dying inside?

And what about how I folded and put away all Sis Goose's things and left them outside Gabe's door? He said nothing, but one day when he was making one of his trips to Indian country to visit friends he'd made there during the war, he took them with him. Didn't I behave with decorum when Granville told Gabe it was time to send me to school and didn't I make the trip down there with Granville without any trouble?

I put up with the silly girls at school, didn't I? I was even sort of a big sister to some of the younger ones. And I even met a young man of good breeding and danced with him and pretended I didn't have a care in the world. Until he confided in me how he unwittingly hurt his brother while rolling around and playing rough on the ground outside.

"He's paralyzed," he confided in me. "And he's my twin."

I didn't tell him about my sin at first. But I accepted an invitation to dinner at his family's home. And now that I'm home again, back from school and teaching the children on our ranch, we write back and forth regularly. Gabe said I could invite him for Christmas. I've told Gabe what happened with Billy and his brother, and he just closed his eyes for a minute and said, "If that's what it takes, Luli, if that's what it takes."

I'm educated now. Among other things I can quote Shakespeare. A good man to quote. All that hatred and killing.

I can, and do, help Mama keep the books. She is retired now but still keeps an eagle eye on things.

The Yankees left in the spring of '69. They didn't leave Texas, no. Our state is still under what they call Reconstruction. Which sometimes turns out to be more of a punishment for Texans than anything. And lots of plantations, including Aunt Sophie's, are still occupied. Gabe rode over there a few times and came home to tell us it was a mess. And there are Aunt Sophie and my sister Amelia, still making their homes in Europe.

I went with Ma and Gabe into our house after the Yankees were gone. The oak floors were scratched. The draperies all torn and ruined, as were the chairs and settles and whatever other furniture was left.

Old rusty guns were on the floor in the dining room. Good dishes were cracked and broken. There were messages left on the walls in paint.

I heard Ma give a little gasp. "Don't worry, Ma, we'll have it fixed up in no time," Gabe promised.

I had already written to Granville in Mexico to bring everything back.

We stayed in the log house until our old house was lovely and beckoned us to live in it again.

Granville even brought back the Thoroughbreds. It is my job to exercise them every day. I guess Gabe thinks I need the fresh air. Either that or he has nobody else to do it properly. And I do it properly, right to the brushing down. I don't need any more scoldings from Gabe. All they do is bruise me and lacerate him.

I gave nobody any trouble. Until the day came for me to move back into the big house, and then I told them no, I'm going to stay.

"What do you mean you're going to stay here in the log house?" Gabe said.

"I feel safe here. All my things are here."

"We'll bring them inside."

I just wanted to be alone. Couldn't they see it? Wasn't I old enough?

"No," Gabe said firmly. "We're a family. There's not much left of us, but what's left is a family. Pa is gone. Granville is gone. Amelia is gone. Sis Goose is gone. There's only us for now, damn it, and we're a family!"

Sis Goose's name hung in the air between us. Nobody talked about her anymore. Her name swung back and forth, hit me in the face, and then hit him.

"No," he said again.

I knew that "no." I grew up with it. "All right," I said. "I'll come."

So I did. But gradually, because I always knew my way around Gabe, I left them. Piece by piece I left them. I'd say I was studying or going over my next day's schoolwork and I needed to use the schoolroom, and I'd burn a lamp late and then fall asleep on the old settle in Pa's study.

Edom died. He must have been over a hundred. We found him dead one day in the back room. It didn't put me off. The place was now all mine. We buried him next to Pa, and now it seemed like all ties to the past were broken.

On those nights when I fell asleep in the study, I'd leave a lamp burning and Gabe would come in and extinguish the lamp and cover me over, and I'd hear words about "you burning the place down and yourself with it" in my dreams.

Every so often Gabe would leave for a few days to take a trip. He had the running of the place mastered. Those days I was to stay in the house with Ma. Strict orders. Sam was in charge but still deferred to Ma. Nobody knew where Gabe went on these trips. But he'd go once every two months or so. And he'd always take some blankets or trinkets for old Indian friends from before the war.

Did he go to San Felipe to visit the nuns and Ham?

Did he go a little farther into that sad little town to visit Sis Goose's grave?

He never said. I knew better than to ask.

What he needed was a woman, I decided. Granville had wired us that he'd taken a wife, a beautiful Mexican girl, and one of these days he'd bring her home to visit.

When he did come home, Gabe always brought some Indian trinkets for me and Ma. He could have passed their reservation along the way.

Finally, I just moved into the log house full time. Nobody said anything. I only went home when Gabe took one of his trips. I fixed the place the way I wanted it, with old rag rugs that Mama gave me. I had the kitchen pots and utensils. Mama let me keep the china from the log house, and on the walls I have drawings the children made me.

My expensive schooling paid off in the end, anyway. And so here I sit in my study and wait. Usually I don't know for what. But this time I do. I am waiting for Gabe to come back from his latest trip. For no reason, except that when he does, I won't have to sleep in the big house anymore and take care of Mama.

It is dusk when he comes. Soon I must go to Mama's for supper. I hear the knock on the front door. He always knocks out of politeness to me. I rush through the gallery, down the hall to the front door. I open it and he is standing there. There is someone with him.

A little boy, about eight years of age. Younger than Ham was when we found him.

He is an Indian boy, though, dressed in leggings and fringed shirt and moccasins, with dark hair and the loveliest brown eyes I ever saw.

I look into Gabe's eyes and for the first time since I shot Sis Goose, his eyes smile back into mine. "Hello, Luli," he says.

I nod and look at the boy.

"This is Sits in the Sun. I brought him to learn at your school."

I nod again, and the little boy extends his hand and I take it. "Hello, Miss Luli," he says.

I gasp. "He speaks English."

Gabe nods. "I've taught him."

They step into the house and I am full of questions, but I know better than to ask. In due time Gabe will talk. And he does, when I bring out some tea and some milk and biscuits for the boy.

The child is looking at the walls, at the drawings of my students.

"Right after he was born, Luli," he says with great difficulty, "I . . . shot his mother in a battle. Never meant to do it. She was running away with him. My shot caught her, and . . ."

"It's all right," I say.

"No, no, it's never all right, honey. We must never mark it as all right. I'm not the father. Want you to know. He's dead. Relatives were raising him. I'd stop by and visit. Bring some things. Keep an eye out. Lately, I've been stopping by a lot. Since my own child was lost."

I let him finish. Let the words crackle with the fire in the hearth and find their way up the chimney to the heavens. That's the only place they could be understood. There and here. In my heart.

I let him finish.

"I'd like you to educate him," he says. Like he needed to ask.

I keep nodding. I would have nodded a yes to the devil himself at the moment. Because all I knew was that what we both needed had just walked through the door in the person of a precious little Indian boy who had nobody to care for him but two broken people looking for a way to get whole again.

"It would be nice," Gabe goes on, "if you'd kind of take over with him. Let Ma be the grandmother. She needs that right now. But for that, you'd have to come and live in the house again. Could you do that, you think?"

The little boy is eating his biscuits and drinking his milk. He smiles at me. "Papa says I have to learn to sleep in a bed," he tells me.

"Papa, is it?" I tease my brother. I won't let him off the hook on that one for a while, you can wager.

Gabe has the decency to blush. "He insists," he says.

"Then let him say it."

We finish our repast. I bring the dishes into the kitchen and wash them. Then I pick up a cloak. It just happens to be the blue velvet, worn from use now. I put it on and go back into the study where they are waiting for me.

"Come on, Sits in the Sun," I say. "Let's go home."

AUTHOR'S NOTE

FOR OVER five years now I've wanted to do a book on Juneteenth, the name given to June 19th, the day in Texas, in 1865, that the slaves finally received their freedom. If you do the math, yes, it is more than two years after the slaves in the East were freed. And if you start to wonder how such a thing came to pass, you can stop wondering. No one I asked can tell me how the Texas ranchers could keep their slaves in bondage while those in the East were free.

As for the book I wanted to do, I could think of no appropriate approach. The subject was as big as the state itself. I knew I had to narrow it down, personalize it. But I could think of no fitting plot. Slavery itself was too big a plot. It would smother me and the reader. No, I had to have a story first. Then I would deal with the history closing in all around it.

Surely this dragging on of slavery hurt a lot of people. I wanted to show how it hurt a precious few, to make my readers care about them.

I wanted to care about them.

Then, early in 2005, the story started to assume shadows against a vast landscape. And I knew right off that it was not a happy landscape. I heard whisperings of my characters, but I did not know yet who they were. I heard angry voices, and I did know that these people had strong convictions, high ideals, traditions to live up to, traditions that might kill them if they didn't watch out. I knew they lived big, like everyone in Texas. I also knew they loved big and hated big. And that included each other. One minute they'd be laughing together, and the next they'd be shooting each other with words as deadly as the guns they were so expert in using.

The story was starting to haunt me.

Basically it would be the story of two girls, one white and one near white, the latter taken in by the family Holcomb as a baby, treated like a princess, while under Texas law still a slave.

The portrait was coming into my sights, huge with its skies and its stars, its flat endless prairie, and its high mountain regions studded with peaks of lime shell and chalky rocks.

I knew I had to bring it to a personalized snapshot, black and white, with all the shadows and gray areas. Only then could I build my story.

For that is how all my historical novels begin. With characters. With their story. Never mind about the history.

Oh, it's there, all right. It's up to me to fit my characters in to this landmark happening. Let it affect the characters' everyday lives. Let them lead me through it.

But wait. It still can't be a story until these characters invite me in.

Some take forever to do this, going about their business and ignoring me.

The characters in this book, it turned out, were there, waiting for me. "Where have you been? We've been waiting five years."

They had the gates of the ranch open, as well as the heavy front door of the house. Did I want a nice cup of coffee? Some of Luli's sugar cookies? Even Gabe and Granville's hound dogs greeted me.

"I'm Luli," a lively, pretty, bursting-with-life teenage girl introduced herself. "And this is Sis Goose."

Sis Goose played her role well. She was older, but shy. Beautiful, but already a woman with secrets.

"And this is my brother Gabe," Luli said, grabbing his elbow with both hands. "My brother Granville is in Mexico. Building empires."

"Mind your manners," Gabe said solemnly. You could see he took responsibility for her, for them all. He took off his planter's hat and smoothed down his brown, sundrenched hair. He was in his midtwenties. Could I do justice to his quiet brand of good looks? Or would mentioning them just demean him? He was so much more than that. A man crowded with obligations, worries, and a river full of memories he had to swim through every day before breakfast.

"Welcome, ma'am," he said to me. "My ma is upstairs taking a nap. She's getting on now, you know."

A dutiful son to Ma, I thought. Yes, I must remember that.

"How's your father?" I asked politely. I knew his father was dying; after all, I'd put him in that upstairs bedroom and given him that stroke.

He turned his planter's hat around in his hands. "Middling well, thanks for asking. Luli, stop jumping around like a possum on a stick."

The girl quieted down. Thirteen, I'd made her thirteen. Impossible age, just to give him trouble. But she minded him. He saw to it. I also saw the fondness in his eyes when he looked at her. As for Sis Goose, there was something else in his eyes when they looked in her direction. *Whoa there, Gabriel,* I thought. *Careful. A person could be as blind as a skunk in daylight and see what you feel for her when your eyes linger there.*

It's come to the point where they are part of me. They generously share their hopes and dreams and fears. I especially know Gabe's fears because he had a laundry list of them, even after he'd fought Kickapoo Indians in the war and come home, his wounds healing better than the guilt he carried.

"I'm afraid of everything," he admitted to his young sister, and he-who-had-fought-Indians sacrificed his macho image to help she-who-was-frightened. Especially, he admitted, sitting down to eat with polite people in polite houses.

"Even ours?" she asked.

And there it is. "Especially ours," says he who has known the cost of the Southern honor his pa schooled them all in. And the heartbreak of living in a house in which everyone is lying to one another one minute and calling each other honey the next. That makes fighting Kickapoo Indians honest at least.

But then, too soon, the story was finished and it was time to leave these people.

Ma gave me a large stone jar of their precious coffee, like the nuns in San Felipe gave Luli, and a thick meat sandwich. "You'll need something to comfort you out there," she said.

How did she know? I didn't ask. Just supposed that her world and mine were different only in the trappings.

But I found the heavy front door locked. And I knew that, even if I could sneak out a window, I would find the gates of the ranch locked against me, too. Somebody didn't want me to leave.

Truth to tell, I didn't want to leave, either. I liked it here.

I stood in the hall, clutching my coffee and sandwich. "I have other books to write," I told them.

"Who locked the door?" Gabe demanded.

Turned out it was Luli. Who else? Sis Goose was long

since gone. Anyway, ghosts can't do such things, can they? Another question: If Sis Goose was long since gone, why was Luli still running around, thirteen years old? Oh, I have to get out of here.

"Do I have to worry about this, too?" Gabe acted irritated, but I knew him well enough to know he liked his role in the family. He must, because other than some gray at the temples he hadn't aged, either. And where was Sits in the Sun, the little Indian boy he brought home? Oh yes, Gabe, do take charge.

"Open the door, Luli," he said. He said it roughly and she cried. Later he'd make it up to her somehow. It was the way of them. They'd fight like brother and sister. She'd sass him. She knew just how far she could go. And he knew how far he should go, and the fragile distance between destroying her and making her strong.

Then in the evening, he'd be lounging in the parlor, talking with Ma about the day's doings of the ranch and having after-supper coffee, his laced with rum, and Luli would come in and sit on the floor next to him and rest her head on his knee. Quiet for a while. Sis Goose would be floating all over that room, haunting Gabe and Luli so they'd both be in pain for what they did to her, for the great lie they told her, for the way they kept her in bondage. Now she would keep them in bondage. Forever.

But Luli has more than that to ponder. What about the great truth she didn't tell Gabe?

"I need a powder, I have a headache," Luli would say.

And she'd get up, but not before sneaking a mouthful of Gabe's coffee.

"Get me one, too," he'd say.

I knew this all because I did it to them. And now I was leaving them with it. If I could only get out that front door.

Luli opened it. Smiled at me through her tears. Kissed me. "He needs a woman," she whispered to me. "Granville's promised to help me find him one."

There's a switch. Her conspiring with Granville.

Gabe nodded to me in the hall. "We're beholden to you, ma'am, for telling our story," he said. "You all come again, now."

I left them there. But at what cost? I know they will never leave me be, that I will always think of them, that they will always have some grip on me, that when I am in the middle of some task or reading a book I will hear Gabe's voice saying, "Why did you make her thirteen? Do you know what she did today?" Or, "Pa is never going to forgive me for Sis Goose."

Or from Luli: "My ma died today. You could have stayed around for that."

Yet I am more fond of them than any characters I ever created. Gabe with his haunted memories and his Southern honor that he upholds and demands so of others. That he knows he can't abandon or he will fall to pieces. Luli with her spirit still intact, though she must fight for it every day. Ma with her quick sharp orders and her own pain near her heart, which only mothers get. And her stern love for her children. And, of course, Sis Goose with her pride and longing to be free.

Thank y'all. I'm beholden.

THE LARGER question my book poses is, how did the Texas ranchers and planters keep the freedom enjoyed by slaves in the East a secret from their own people in bondage?

The "how" is a mystery, except to say that most Texas farms and ranches and plantations were worlds unto themselves, as was Texas itself. Communication from establishment to establishment was likely at a minimum, and the level of information given to slaves kept under a tight rein.

Of course the slaves knew there was a war on. They called it the freedom war. But they did not know the battles, the wins and losses, or the particulars. They sang about it, they prayed about it, they dreamed about freedom, but most never expected it in their lifetime.

As for their white owners, their biggest reason for keeping their slaves ignorant of the freedom enjoyed by their brothers and sisters in the East was the slave labor. After that it was because they feared if their slaves knew of it there would be a slave uprising.

They constantly feared a slave uprising.

During the Civil War, Texas was called "the dark corner of the Confederacy" by many, simply because Texas wanted to be left alone, to govern itself, not to be intruded upon by outsiders, and because there was so much land yet unexplored, land that went on for miles and miles, land yet occupied only by Indians.

Yet during the war, Texas was the largest producer of cotton in the Confederacy. New England textile manufacturers, running low on cotton, wanted President Lincoln to order an invasion of Texas. But Lincoln ignored them.

Indeed, though there were Federal troops in Texas during the war, there was no wholesale invasion of the state by the Union. Homes and personal properties were not destroyed and occupied as they were back east.

Some Texas army units, like Gabe's, spent all of the war in the state, assigned to defend the frontier against the Indians. Others fought with General Robert E. Lee, and still others went into battle east of the Mississippi.

There was a Federal blockade of the Texas coast in July 1861, which was a death knell for Texas commerce and for Texas cotton merchants. But soon enterprising Texas businessmen and planters (like Luli's brother Granville) discovered a loophole in the blockade by shipping cotton through Bagdad, Mexico.

The incident in the book about coyotes eating the shoes and hats of Gabe and Luli was adapted from an incident in the book *Pioneering in Texas: True Stories of the Early Days* by Winnie Allen, archivist, University of Texas, and Corrie Walker Allen, adjunct professor of education, University of Texas, The Southern Publishing Company, 1935. All the stories in that book were adapted from original sources. Everything else in *Come Juneteenth* is a product of my own imagination.

The name Sis Goose goes back to an animal tale in the style of the Brer Fox and Brer Rabbit stories of Joel Chandler Harris. Collected from the oral tradition and written down by A. W. Eddins, a San Antonio schoolteacher, the tale reads: "En so dey went to cote [court] and when dey got dere, de sheriff, he wus er fox, en de judge, he wus er fox, en all de jurymen, dey wus foxes, too. En dey tried ole Sis Goose, en dey 'victed her en dey 'scuted her, en dey picked her bones."

Reconstruction was the formal name given to the military takeover by Federal troops of Confederate states after the war was over. It lasted, in some states, from 1865 to the 1870s. General Gordon Granger came to Texas to issue the Emancipation Proclamation for Texas slaves on June 19, 1865.

In many cases, Yankees occupied Confederate plantations and ranches like they did in my book, taking over the big house, running the place, and ordering the white folk around. Actually they were there to see that the Southerners properly freed their slaves and were living up to the law of the land. Some simply took advantage of their situation, living high off the hog. Many behaved like gentleman and kept things in line but, unfortunately, too many played their roles to the hilt and made things miserable for the Southerners.

There was no specific time for them to leave. Many did not leave until the midseventies and many left the premises they had occupied in a dreadful state. But the Southerners were lucky if they did not come on strong, shooting the cattle and dogs and horses, burning the barn and houses.

Reconstruction, for many Southerners, was indeed a sad chapter in our history.

Within a short time after the slaves in Texas were freed, there was established a whole spectrum of celebration that became known as Juneteenth to celebrate that 19th of June in 1865 when the Texas slaves finally received their freedom. It is celebrated to this day.

BIBLIOGRAPHY

Abernethy, Francis Edward, Patrick B. Mullen, and Alan B. Govenar. *Juneteenth Texas: Essays in African-American Folklore.* Denton, Texas: University of North Texas Press, 1996.

Adams, George Washington. *Doctors in Blue: The Medical History of the Union Army in the Civil War.* Dayton, Ohio: Morningside, 1985.

Allen, Winnie, and Allen, Corrie Walker, *Pioneering in Texas: True Stories of the Early Days.* Dallas, Texas: The Southern Publishing Company, 1935.

Exley, Jo Ella Powell, Editor. *Texas Tears and Texas Sunshine: Voices of Frontier Women.* College Station, Texas: Texas A & M University Press, 1985.

Foner, Eric. *Reconstruction: America's Unfinished Revolution, 1863–1877.* New York, NY: Harper & Row, 1988.

Gallaway, B.P., Ed. *Texas: The Dark Corner of the Confederacy.* Lincoln, Nebraska: University of Nebraska Press, 1994.

Holley, Mary Austin. *Texas.* Austin, Texas: The Texas State Historical Association, 1990.

Massey, Mary Elizabeth. *Ersatz in the Confederacy: Shortages and Substitutes on the Southern Homefront.* Columbia, SC: University of South Carolina, 1952.

McLeRoy, Sherrie S. *Red River Women: Women of the West.* Plano, Texas: Wordware Publishing Inc., 1996.

Nagel, Paul C. *The Lees of Virginia: Seven Generations of an American Family.* New York, Oxford: Oxford University Press, 1990.

Pinckney, Roger. *Blue Roots: African-American Folk Magic of the Gullah People.* St. Paul, Minnesota: Llewellyn Publications, 1998.

Seagraves, Anne. *High-Spirited Women of the West.* Hayden, Idaho: Wesanne Publications, 1992.

Silverthorne, Elizabeth. *Plantation Life in Texas.* College Station, Texas: Texas A & M University Press, 1986.

Tyler, Ron, and Lawrence R. Murphy, Eds. *The Slave Narratives of Texas.* Austin, Texas: The Encino Press, 1974.